D0590568

what are
the odds?

what are the odds?

THE ODDS ON EVERYTHING BOOK

Graham Sharpe and Roger L. Schlaifer

Copyright © Graham Sharpe and Roger L. Schlaifer 2007
Published by arrangement with the Bantam Dell Publishing Group,
a division of Random House, Inc.

The right of Graham Sharpe and Roger L. Schlaifer
to be identified as the authors of this work
has been asserted by them in accordance with the
Copyright, Designs and Patents Act 1988.

First published in hardback in Great Britain in 2007 by
Orion Books
an imprint of the Orion Publishing Group Ltd
Orion House, 5 Upper St Martin's Lane,
London WC2H 9EA
An Hachette Livre UK Company

10 9 8 7 6 5 4 3 2 1

A CIP catalogue record for this book is available
from the British Library.

ISBN: 978 0 7528 7597 2

Printed in Great Britain by Clays Ltd, St Ives plc

Illustrations by Gordon Thompson

The Orion Publishing Group's policy is to use papers that are natural,
renewable and recyclable and made from wood grown in sustainable
forests. The logging and manufacturing processes are expected to
conform to the environmental regulations of the country of origin.

Every effort has been made to fulfil requirements with regard to
reproducing copyright material. The authors and publisher will be glad
to rectify any omissions at the earliest opportunity.

www.orionbooks.co.uk

Contents

To anyone who won't immediately think,
'Oh no, not another book by him!'

Graham Sharpe

In memory of Dad ...
For inspiring me with his generosity, good
humour and endless curiosity.

Roger L. Schlaifer

Introduction

What are the odds that you know the first time the word 'odds' was used in a betting sense? We would say at least 500/1, unless you are a Shakespeare scholar. The Bard introduced the word into common parlance in *Henry IV*, when a character declares, 'I will lay oddes, that ere the yeere expire, We beare our Civill Swords ... as farre as France.' We bet you didn't know that.

Odds are just another way of expressing in mathematical terms the likelihood or otherwise of a named event coming to pass. Odds of 'ten to one', or 10/1, represent a one in eleven chance of something happening. So if you bet £1 at odds of 10/1 at a bookie's, you would win ten times your stake money – £10 – and get back your stake, giving a total return of £11 for your initial outlay of £1.

We know it takes a little effort to grasp the concept, which always seems to be the case where percentages, proportions and odds are concerned. In 1998 a German survey conducted by the Emnid Institute asked 1,000 people what 40% meant. Was it 'one-quarter'; '4 out of 10'; or 'every 40th'? Approximately a third of the respondents got it wrong. Hopefully, though, after reading this book, you will have a better understanding of odds and percentages.

'One in eleven' means that for every eleven potential outcomes, one will take place, while the ten others will not. It is an alternative way of describing odds – as are percentages.

A 10% chance equates to odds of 9/1, and means that where there is a 100% chance that something either WILL or WILL NOT happen, it is estimated (usually by a bookie, possibly by an insurance agent) that there is a 10% chance of one of those options and a 90% chance of the other.

Confused? Don't be. You'll get the hang of it soon enough. To help you out, here's a little chart to explain the various ways of expressing the *same* thing:

Odds	Percentages	One in ... chance
6/4	40%	One in two and a half (or two in five)
2/1	33.33%	One in three
3/1	25%	One in four
4/1	20%	One in five
10/1	9.09%	One in eleven

Now you are ready to tackle the challenges that lie ahead – and it's an odds-on shot that you'll be amused, enraged, outraged and entertained by the answers to our hundreds of trivial yet intriguing factoids from everyday life.

LIFE OR DEATH

'It's not that I'm afraid of dying, I just don't want to be around when it happens.'

Woody Allen

Scalpel, Forceps, Embalming Fluid

YOU'RE MOST **likely to die from which of the following surgeries?**

A) Liposuction   **B)** Hernia   **C)** Hip Replacement

_____

Bagged by Your Dry Cleaner

YOUR LIFETIME **chance of being suffocated by a plastic laundry bag is which of the following?**

A) 1 in 3,000   **B)** 1 in 13,000   **C)** 1 in 130,000

_____

What the Hell?

WHAT PERCENTAGE **of people believe that members of thir family will go to Hell?**

A) 25%   **B)** 54%   **C)** 61%

LIFE OR DEATH

3

ANSWERS . . . .

C) Hip Replacement

Of the 120,000 hip replacements performed annually, about 400 patients die from complications within three months of the surgery – most often because of the advanced age of the patient. Liposuction sucks the fat – and the life – out of about 80 people annually. Hernia surgery, though a pain in the groin, is responsible for only an estimated 40 deaths out of the 800,000 procedures done annually.

Source: Center for Disease Control (CDC) (2004)

C) 1 in 130,000

There's no reason to end up with a tag on your toe instead of your jacket, but each year 27 people turn up as stiff as their own starched shirts by not taking those clingy clothes wraps seriously enough. Turns out mob money isn't the only thing it's dangerous to launder.

Source: CDC (2004)

A) 25%

61% of males questioned said that they knew someone who would end up in Hell. 54% of females answered likewise, but 25% of all respondents believed that they had family members headed towards Satan's sanctuary.

Source: Online survey of 10,000 members of www.beliefnet.com

Hey, Guys? We're Out of Peanuts!'

WHEN THE Uruguay rugby team crashed into the Andes in 1972, what was the chance of a survivor of the ordeal staying alive by eating the flesh of other, dead passengers?

A) 25%   **B)** 50%   **C)** 100%

Look! Up in the Sky! It's . . . OW!

WHAT IS your lifetime chance of being killed by a falling object?

A) 1 in 4,900   **B)** 1 in 49,000   **C)** 1 in 490,000

Fumes-Day Scenario

WHAT IS your lifetime chance of *accidentally* dying in a car from motor-vehicle exhaust?

A) 1 in 7,000   **B)** 1 in 11,000   **C)** 1 in 19,000

LIFE OR DEATH

ANSWERS . . . .

C) 100%

Spending 71 days lost and without food in the snow-covered Andes made the unthinkable thinkable, and ultimately doable, as the 16 rugby players who survived clearly showed. But none of the agony they went through prepared them for the really brutal ordeal of having to watch Ethan Hawke and Vince Spano play them in the movie.

Source: Piers Paul Read, *Alive*

A) 1 in 4,900

When someone dies suddenly, it may seem to come 'out of thin air', but a particularly unlucky group experiences that sensation a bit more literally. Just over 700 people are struck and killed by falling objects each year. (Those struck by falling apples are more likely to survive – and have scientific epiphanies!)

Source: NSC (2004)

C) 1 in 19,000

About 190 people a year are gassed accidentally in their own cars – and that number doesn't even include the ill effects of those dangling air 'fresheners'. The moral here would seem to be: don't leave your engine running – even for a chance to get lucky in the back seat.

Source: NSC (2004)

A Real Sinking Feeling

WHAT'S your lifetime chance of drowning?

A) 1 in 900   **B)** 1 in 9,000   **C)** 1 in 90,000

Ciao via Plough

YOUR LIFETIME chance of being killed by a bulldozer, earthmover or other excavating equipment is:

A) 1 in 4,500   **B)** 1 in 45,000   **C)** 1 in 450,000

Butting Out

WHICH of the following digestive disorders is *least* likely to kill you?

A) Constipation   **B)** Haemorrhoids   **C)** Diarrhoea

LIFE OR DEATH

7

A) 1 in 900

Better hang on to those water-wings! About 3,300 people a year end up in Davy Jones's locker. Of these, about 600 meet their maker in pools, 1,000 in natural bodies of water and about 300 in bathtubs; the rest are lumped into an 'unspecified' category of drownings. Wells? Buckets? Finger bowls?

Source: NSC (2003)

B) 1 in 45,000

The serious downside of buildings going up is that around 80 people a year go under from unfortunate encounters with earthmovers. On the upside, it could save your family a bundle on burial costs.

Source: NSC (2004)

A) Haemorroids

Pile on all the jokes you want, apparently almost nobody (well, only 16) dies from haemorroids and the embarrassment they might cause. That number nearly doubles to 28 for the three million constipation sufferers in the US.

Source: NDDIC; NIH (2004)

Postcards from the Ledge

WHAT'S THE chance of a suicide victim leaving a note?

A) 1 in 6   **B)** 1 in 8   **C)** 1 in 10

From 'FU' to RIP

WHAT'S THE chance that a road-rage incident in the US will end in someone's death?

A) 1 in 350   **B)** 1 in 1,100   **C)** 1 in 2,700

Ghost of a chance

WHAT PERCENTAGE of people believe they have seen a ghost?

A) 9%   **B)** 13%   **C)** 25%

LIFE OR DEATH

9

A) 1 in 6

With fewer than 20% of victims leaving a note, you'll probably never know exactly what made them do it. (Although the 63 new voicemail messages from debt collection agencies could be a clue.)

Source: FriendsforSurvival.org

B) 1 in 1,100

Think twice before giving the finger to that idiot trying to pass you on the inside. It's hardly going to change your life – but it might if you antagonise him. There have been more than 200 deaths and 12,600 injuries attributed to road rage in the US since 1990.

Source: AAA (2004)

C) 25%

Nine per cent of people polled believe themselves to be psychic – which makes you wonder why the person doing the survey would have needed to ask them any questions before being given the answers. 13% apparently believe they can 'affect machinery or electronic equipment' with their mysterious powers, and 25% claim to have seen a ghost

Source: Access/BMRB for Reader's Digest (May 2006)

WHAT ARE THE ODDS?

Who Ordered the Stake?

IF YOU were arrested for witchcraft during the infamous Salem witch-hunt and trials of 1692, what were your chances of being executed?

A) 1 in 4   **B)** 1 in 8   **C)** 1 in 20

Emergency Admissions

ACCIDENTS WILL happen – and falls, crashes and medical emergencies are expected to put people into A&E wards. But which of the following is more likely to precipitate a visit to hospital?

A) Curtain Pelmets   **B)** Clothes Pegs   **C)** Cardigans

LIFE OR DEATH

Dead Loss?

WHAT ARE the odds that a football fan would miss a family funeral to attend a match?

A) 20/1   **B)** 8/1   **C)** 3/1

11

B) 1 in 8

Over 150 people were arrested for witchcraft during this period of mass hysteria. Of those, twenty were executed, three died in prison and an 80-year-old man was 'pressed to death' by heavy stones. Two escaped – whether as bats or cats is not known – and a couple of dogs were executed, just in case.

Source: salemwitchcrafttrials.com (2004)

C) Cardigans

There were 900,000 admissions to English hospitals attributable to accidents during 2005. Of these, 123 were caused by curtain pelmets, 431 were due to those vicious clothes pegs and an amazing 964 were cardigan calamities.

Source: *Daily Mirror* (10 January 2006)

C) 3/1

'Such is the respect some fans have for the game that one in four said they would miss a family funeral to watch a match,' reported a frankly disgusted *Daily Express* in March 2006. Mind you, I have attended many matches at Kenilworth Road, home of my beloved Luton Town FC, which could have doubled up as family funerals.

Source: Survey for Duracell (March 2006)

Leaving Home

WHAT ARE the odds that you will die at home?

A) Evens   **B)** 4/1   **C)** 16/1

Upon My Soul

WHAT PERCENTAGE of people believe that their soul or spirit will continue to exist after death?

A) 5%   **B)** 29%   **C)** 46%

Can't Live with Her

WHAT ARE the chances that a man aged between 25 and 50 who divorces his wife will die before his still-married contemporaries?

A) Half as Likely   **B)** As Likely   **C)** Twice as Likely

LIFE OR DEATH

B) 4/1

Over two-thirds of people say they would like to die at home, but only one in five actually manages it. According to a survey of 1,500 people, 33% of heart patients and 33% of those dying from old age experienced a 'good death'. Excuse me? How do they know?

Source: *How to Have a Good Death* (BBC TV, March 2006)

B) 29%

Of the 761 Britons who responded to a survey, 5% felt that 'souls don't survive but my life force may go on in some form'; 46% grimly thought, 'I'm fairly sure that nothing will survive my death'; and 20% admitted that they didn't have a clue what was going to happen. That leaves just under a third who think, 'Part of me, what's called my soul or spirit, will continue to exist in an afterlife.'

Source: *The Times* (15 April 2006)

C) Twice as Likely

So any man who tells you he is just dying to get divorced might be speaking literally!

Source: *The Times* (15 April 2006)

Life Begins At, er . . .

THE PUBLICATION of the 1841 census online in 2006 revealed that average life expectancy for a man in those days was:

A) 40.2 Years **B)** 42.2 Years **C)** 44.4 Years

The Hippocratic Oaf

WHAT IS your chance of dying from a medical complication due to surgical mistake or other medical care?

A) 1 in 1,100 **B)** 1 in 5,500 **C)** 1 in 11,000

Grave Concern

WHAT PERCENTAGE of people, asked to name the one thing they would like to take with them to their grave, opted for their mobile phone?

A) 3% **B)** 24% **C)** 39%

LIFE OR DEATH

15

A) 40.2 Years

Life may begin at 40 today, but when Victoria was on the throne men enjoyed only another couple of months after that milestone. The Queen herself managed to keep going for quite a while longer, of course, as did all women, who on average made it to 42.2. Fifteen per cent of babies didn't even make it to their first birthday.

Source: 1841 Census

A) 1 in 1,100

No wonder they call it 'practising' medicine; in the US it is estimated that there are 44,000 to 98,000 deaths a year attributable to medical errors.

Source: NSC (2004)

B) 24%

Top choice of burial accessory was sentimental – jewellery/wedding rings – voted for by 39%. Also popular were photographs, letters and childhood toys (3% went for their teddy bear). But almost a quarter chose their mobile phone to accompany them on their final journey. Maybe they think St Peter will accept texted answers to save time at the Pearly Gates, although a more popular reason given for their seemingly peculiar choice was that it would get them out of a bit of a pickle if they were buried alive.

Source: Dial-a-Phone pay-as-you-go survey (April 2006)

HEALTH & HAPPINESS

'Oh come on, do I look like I'm dying? I'm sorry, folks, I'm not dead and I don't plan on it.'

74-year-old Elizabeth Taylor, May 2006

Dental Dreaming

WHAT ARE the odds that you will dream about your teeth falling out?

A) 10/1   **B)** 8/1   **C)** 5/2

Undercover Activity

OTHER THAN sleeping, the chance is 1 in 5 that you will be doing which of the following in bed tonight?

A) Smoking   **B)** Snoring   **C)** Having Sex

Unhealthy Reasoning

WHAT PERCENTAGE of men claimed that the cost of healthy food was their prime reason for failing to adopt a healthy diet?

A) 19%   **B)** 23%   **C)** 24%

HEALTH & HAPPINESS

19

B) 8/1

One in eleven of those surveyed had dreamed about flying, which apparently symbolises rising above a situation; two in seven dreamed of being chased – running away from something; and one in nine dreamed of dental drama, which is supposed to reflect an anxiety about appearance. Sounds more like a nightmare.

Source: Survey of 2,500 people conducted by Heinz (2007)

B) Snoring

While fewer folks puff on the pillows these days, it is estimated that 20% of adults snore at night. Since the typical snorer is overweight, has high blood pressure and has consumed alcohol shortly before bedtime, is it any wonder that the chance of the average adult having sex is less than 1 in 6?

Source: CDC; NCHS (2004)

C) 24%

19% claimed that being too busy at work was what stopped them concentrating on healthy eating while 23% confessed to a lack of willpower, but 24% claimed somewhat dubiously that the cost was to blame – like fruit is more expensive than junk food!

Source: Survey of 5,016 people by YouGov for Sainsbury's (2007)

ANSWERS ➤

Eye, Caramba!

WHAT PERCENTAGE of 50-year-olds develop presbyopia – trouble seeing things close up?

A) Over 35%   **B)** Over 75%   **C)** Over 95%

A Walk in the Dark

A SLEEPWALKING episode is most likely to last approximately how long?

A) 6 Seconds   **B)** 60 Seconds   **C)** 6 Minutes

Out of Sight

WHAT ARE the chances that a blind person was born without sight?

A) 90%   **B)** 60%   **C)** 35%

HEALTH & HAPPINESS

ANSWERS . . . .

C) Over 95%

Bring out the bifocals and grab a cane. Almost everyone will have trouble seeing close up as they age. It's
due to a hardening of the lens inside the eye, and it
affects men and women equally. Most will compensate
by increasing the length of their arms. If you think
that's funny, you must be under 40. Just you wait.

Source: NIH (2004)

C) 6 Minutes

A very fit somnambulist would therefore have enough
time to run a mile. However, if you bump into a 'sleep-
walker' whose flesh seems to be rotting off his body as
he moans, 'Brains ... brains,' you might want to do a
little running yourself.

Source: health.allrefer.com

C) 35%

The blinding truth is that most unsighted people
weren't always that way. Of the two-thirds born
sighted, at least half lose their eyesight due to disease,
and most of the others due to injury. (The moral?
Eyesight is a gift, so don't take it for granted. You
know, like you did with your sex life before you got
married.)

Source: Provident Medical Institute 2001; AAFP (1998)

ANSWERS ➤

Don't Be Rash . . .

ALLERGY SUFFERERS are most likely to be allergic to which of the following fruits?

A) Bananas   **B)** Apples   **C)** Pears

Fit for Purpose?

IN THE UK's biggest ever survey of exercise levels, what percentage of adults admitted doing no exercise whatsoever?

A) 6.3%   **B)** 21%   **C)** 50%

The Sum of the Parts

IF YOU'RE an average, healthy person who dies in an accident, odds are you could help up to how many people by being an organ donor?

A) 25   **B)** 50   **C)** 110

HEALTH & HAPPINESS

ANSWERS . . . .

A) Bananas

Allergy sufferers may experience cross-reactivity, which makes them allergic to certain fruits. Of these, bananas are among the most common. An overwhelming desire to hang from trees and beat one's chest frantically is a giveaway symptom.

Source: American Academy of Allergy, Asthma and Immunology (2002)

C) 50%

The survey covered 364,00 people in 354 local authority regions and revealed that only 21% of the adult population could claim the minimum level of exercise recommended – three half an hour sessions per week of moderate intensity sport or active recreation. But half of those surveyed indulged in no significant exercise at all. Only 6.3% exercised daily.

Source: Survey by Ipsos Mori for Sport England (December 2006)

B) 50

Since everything from hearts to corneas can now be successfully transplanted, a single donor could help as many as 50 other folks. An impressive 55% of the adult US population list themselves as donors, with a few brave, living donors giving nonessential kidneys and bone marrow.

Source: NWIHC; ABCNews.com (2003)

Losers

THE PHYSICAL **prowess of most men peaks in their late teens or early 20s. If you're a guy approaching 40, you're most likely to experience which of the following?**

A) Hair Loss   **B)** Hearing Loss   **C)** Erectile Dysfunction

---

Coke Kids

WHAT PROPORTION **of British 11–15-year-olds have tried cocaine?**

A) 0.5%   **B)** 2%   **C)** 5%

Wake-up Call

HOW MANY **Britons get less than five hours' sleep a night?**

A) One in Three   **B)** One in Six   **C)** One in Nine

ANSWERS . . . .

A) **Hair Loss**

Yep! Fall out is probably your worst problem – at least for now – with 25 to 30% of men balding or seriously shedding by the time they're in their 20s. Despite what your mother said, hearing loss affects only about 14% of men in or near their 40s, and erectile dysfuntion only about 5 to 10% – unless you are a heavy drinker or smoker, which could mean that it is all downhill from here.

Source: NHS (2002)

B) **2%**

The most dangerous substance anyone used to consume at my school was free milk that had been left out in the sun too long, but those days are long gone. According to one official study, carried out among 9,000 pupils from 305 schools, 'cocaine use among 11–15-year-olds doubled from 1% to 2% between 2004 and 2005'.

Source: *The Times* (25 March 2006)

A) **One in Three**

A poll of 7,000 people revealed that only two out of every three people get the bare minimum five hours' sleep each night. A mere 19% sleep for the recommended eight hours. One per cent claimed to be kept awake 'by their bedfellow breaking wind'.

Source: GMTV (2006)

Pregnant Pause

WHAT PERCENTAGE of Scottish women smoke during pregnancy?

A) 24%   **B)** 13%   **C)** 7%

Stomach Ache

WHAT ARE the odds that an adult male will be unhappy with the state of his stomach?

A) 2/1   **B)** 4/1   **C)** 6/1

Ecstatic About That?

HOW MANY Britons between the ages of 15 and 34 admit to having taken ecstasy?

A) 1 in 10   **B)** 1 in 25   **C)** 1 in 40

HEALTH & HAPPINESS

A) 24%

While it might at least prevent them from snacking on battered Mars bars, it seems that almost a quarter of Scots simply can't give up the fags, no matter who may suffer because of it.

Source: *The Times* (27 March 2006)

A) 2/1

A fifth of men are unhappy with their legs, and a quarter admit to having problems with their entire body, according to a survey of 500 men conducted by Norwich Union Healthcare, which also revealed that 'a third of men hate their stomachs'. The survey suggested that the ideal male-body role model is David Beckham, Brad Pitt or Gavin Henson. (No mention was made of the mind.)

Source: *Marketing Week* (March 2006)

A) 1 in 10

In April 2006 it was reported that a 37-year-old man from London, who had begun using ecstasy when he was 21, had taken a record 40,000 pills in a nine-year period before quitting. Can't think he achieved too much during his 20s.

Source: *Evening Standard* (4 April 2006)

A Little Wrong in the Tooth

FOR THE over-65 crowd, having teeth has replaced having tobacco as something to chew on. What are the chances that anyone in this age bracket has full or partial dentures?

A) 80%   **B)** 60%   **C)** 40%

What's Up, Doc? I Said, What's Up, Doc?

WHAT PERCENTAGE of GPs' patients are 'completely unable to understand the answers' they are given when they ask their doctor a question?

A) 2%   **B)** 9%   **C)** 22%

Not Having a Ball!

HEY, GUYS! If you discover a lump where your balls should be – and it turns out to be cancer – you are most likely to have which of the following procedures?

A) Radiation Treatment   **B)** One Gonad Removed
C) Two Gonads Removed

HEALTH & HAPPINESS

29

B) 60%

For the more than 35 million senior citizens in the US, losing most, if not all, of your teeth is nothing to laugh about. In addition, poorly fitting dentures greatly exacerbate more serious problems, since not chewing properly is one of the leading cuases of choking deaths. Makes you want to floss a little more fervently, doesn't it?

Source: NHANESIII

A) 2%

Reportedly, 75% of GPs' patients get answers they can 'definitely understand'; 22% get answers they can 'mostly understand'; and 2% are 'completely unable' to understand the answers. One per cent claim never to have been given the opportunity to ask any questions! I'm not sure how to assess the answer I got from my doctor when I reported in with a lump on my knee and asked him what he thought it was. After several minutes of poking, prodding, umming and aahing, he answered, 'I think you've got a lump on your knee.'

Source: Healthcare Commission Primary Care Trust Survey of Patients 2005

B) One Gonad Removed

You'll be relieved to know that in most cases, only one has to go. And, the cure rate for testicular cancer, when treated early, is about 95%. So remember, while you're down there take time to check for lumps. The prospect of having your nuts cut off isn't a good one, but dying to keep them is even worse. Do it right, and you might be touring France with Lance Armstrong.

Source: NCI; SEER (2004) TCRC (2004)

Just a Minute – Let Me Worry About My Body

WHAT PERCENTAGE of women claim to worry about their size and shape 'every waking minute'?

A) 29%   **B)** 41%   **C)** 98%

_____

Breast of Both Worlds

WHAT PERCENTAGE of UK women having cosmetic surgery will have it on their breasts?

A) 12%   **B)** 22%   **C)** 34%

_____

Depressing Results

WHAT PROPORTION of people told researchers that they experience bouts of depression or anxiety?

A) One-quarter   B) Two-thirds   C) Three-quarters

HEALTH & HAPPINESS

31

ANSWERS . . . .

A) 29%

A survey of 5,000 women (average age 34) indicated that 2% of women are happy with the shape of their body, whereas 41% are 'constantly on a diet'. The 'average' woman worries about her body every 15 minutes, but '29% worry about their size and shape every waking minute'. The survey didn't bother asking men's opinions, because the result would be a foregone conclusion: 100% of heterosexual males worry about women's bodies 100% of the time.

Source: *Grazia* (April 2006)

C) 34%

Of those, 12% want reduction while 22% opt for 'augmentation'. The latter figure is jointly the most frequently chosen cosmetic surgery, along with dentistry, with Botox taking third place (20% of all treatments).

Source: *Daily Record* (13 April 2006)

B) Two-thirds

Some 2,032 people were consulted in a survey organised by Mintel/YouGov for the British Association for Counselling and Psychotherapy (BACP). Of those who suffered depression, 44% blamed relationship problems and almost as many pressure of work. The most likely age group to admit to depression was the 35–44s, of whom 72% said they suffered depression or anxiety. How depressing is all this? I think I'm beginning to get depressed just thinking about it.

Source: *Body & Soul* (15 April 2006)

Old Women Rule, OK?

AS THE **Queen celebrated her 80th birthday on 21 April 2006, it was revealed that what percentage of people in Britain aged 80 or over are women?**

A) 49%   **B)** 57%   **C)** 65%

How Likely is Fat?

WHAT PERCENTAGE **of the UK population can be classified as 'obese'?**

A) 14%   **B)** 23%   **C)** 30.6%

Shooting Blanks

IF YOU'RE **a guy wanting to have kids, enthusiasm and all the right operating equipment might not be enough. What are the chances that a male will be the infertile member of the couple?**

A) 10%   **B)** 20%   **C)** 40%

HEALTH & HAPPINESS

C) 65%

Not that I'm biased, but men work longer hours and retire later, so it's hardly surprising that nearly twice as many women make it to their ninth decade, is it?

Source: *Daily Mail* (18 April 2006)

B) 23%

In a Chunky Top 10, the Czech Republic took 10th place with 14.8% of its population classified as obese, while the UK wobbled in at number 3, just behind Mexico (with 24.2%). Of course, the runaway winner (albeit a purple-faced and out-of-breath one) was the US with 30.6%.

Source: *Daily Record* (18 April 2006)

C) 40%

Guys can hump themselves silly, but male infertility is responsible for 40% or more of couples' infertility. The variety of causes include low, or no, sperm count, an obstruction, or something called 'retrograde ejaculation' – that's when the little guys swim in the wrong direction ending up in the bladder, where, if they are not immediately recovered, they get *really pissed*.

Source: National Center for Health Statistics (2001)

LOVE & MARRIAGE

'Marriage is like putting your hand into a bag of snakes in the hope of pulling out an eel.'

Leonardo Da Vinci

Oh No We Don"t

WHAT PERCENTAGE of couples in their first marriage say they argue once or twice a week?

A) 11%   **B)** 14%   **C)** 21%

How Many Times?

FOR SOME, the honeymoon never ends. What are the odds that a married couple is sexually 'engaged' four or more times a week?

A) 3%   **B)** 7%   **C)** 11%

Matching Pairs?

IF A woman has already had one set of fraternal twins without artificial help, what are her chances of having another set, compared to the average woman?

A) Twice as Likely   **B)** 4 Times as Likely   **C)** 6 Times as Likely

LOVE & MARRIAGE

37

B) 14%

21% of cohabiting couples, 11% of second marriage couples and 14% of first marriage couples are at each other's throats once or twice a week, while 16% of first-timers claim never to argue. Yeah, right.

Source: YouGov survey on behalf of the *Sunday Times* (2006)

B) 7%

Guess we can call those 7% 'lucky in love'! But 43% of men and 47% of women say they're in action only a 'few times' a month; and 3% of women and 1% of men say they do without *entirely*.

Source: NCI; SEER (2004); TCRC (2004)

B) 4 Times as Likely

Women who bear fraternal twins often have a pattern of releasing more than one egg per cycle, and therefore have a better chance of having another set – a great shortcut to your own in-house football team, although a bit overwhelming when contemplating university fees later on.

Source: www.about.com; www.nomotci.org (2003)

Tell-a-Tubby

WHO IS least likely to recognise that a child is obese?

A) Dad   **B)** Mum   **C)** Doctor

Have You Met the Old Girl?

IN 1963 15% of married British women had younger husbands. What was the percentage by 2003?

A) 14%   **B)** 22%   **C)** 26%

Toyboys – or Girls

WHAT PERCENTAGE of women in England or Wales marrying for the first time will be aged under 30?

A) 60%   **B)** 40%   **C)** 25%

LOVE & MARRIAGE

ANSWERS . . . .

A) Dad

According to a British study, a third of mums but 57% of dads failed to recognise that their little (or large) ones were anything other than perfect.

Source: www.MSNBC.com

C) 26%

Cradle-snatching is clearly a booming pastime for women as well as men.

Source: Office for National Statistics Social Trends Report (February 2006)

B) 40%

The average age at which a woman weds is 30 years and 7 months; the average age for a man is 32 years and 10 months. But only 4 out of 10 women marry before they turn 30. These days, not only Cyndi Lauper wants to have fun.

Source: Office for National Statistics (March 2006)

That Trophy Time of Wife?

SOME THINK of it as 'trading up' and for others it's the only way to get it up. What's the chance that a man over 45 will divorce his wife to marry a much younger woman?

A) 1 in 5   **B)** 1 in 10   **C)** 1 in 45

House Husbands

WHAT ARE the chances of a British man admitting that he rarely or never does housework?

A) 61%   **B)** 22%   **C)** 8%

In Love Online?

WHAT PERCENTAGE of users of www.match.com are aged 45–59, the fastest growing age group seeking partners on the internet dating site?

A) 11%   **B)** 22%   **C)** 33%

LOVE & MARRIAGE

B) 1 in 10

Those new models in the showroom can sure turn a guy's head especially if the old model hasn't been given a good service. Of course, the cost of one of those zippy new things can be prohibitively expensive by the time you pay to get rid of the old one and do what you'll have to do to keep the new one running smoothly.

Source: American Sexual Behavour, National Opinion Research Centre (1998)

B) 22%

If I only knew how to work a washing machine or iron I might be prepared to use one, but count me among the 22% of British men who never get involved in household chores. The Swedes leave us standing or, more accurately, sitting, as only 8% of them don't help around the home, but we are slightly more active than the table-tapping, but never table-wiping, Portuguese, of whom 61% expect someone else to do such jobs.

Source: European Social Survey (2006)

B) 22%

A spokeswoman for a rival site, Yahoo Personals, suggests that this age group is becoming especially keen on cyber-romance because they have seen their children using the internet to get dates. Really? My kids won't even let me into their bedrooms, let alone allow me to see what they get up to on their PCs!

Source: www.match.com (March 2006)

Women Are Secsier Than Men

HOW MANY women make up their minds about whether a man represents a potential partner within 30 seconds of meeting him?

A) 22%   **B)** 33%   **C)** 45%

D.I.Y.U.S.O.B

WHAT PERCENTAGE of couples argue over delays in completing DIY jobs?

A) 81%   **B)** 55%   **C)** 21%

On Wife Support

BASED ON past experience, the champion of the World Wife-Carrying Championships is most likely to be from which country?

A) Estonia   **B)** Malta   **C)** Tonga

LOVE & MARRIAGE

C) **45%**

Analysis of 100 people engaging in 500 'speed dates' revealed that in a third of cases participants made up their minds about whether they were attracted to their opposite number in less than 30 seconds, but that broke down into just 22% of the men and 45% of the women. When I first met my wife, it took me a nanosecond to decide that I fancied her and, at the time of writing, 35 years to debate whether that was a correct decision.

Source: Study by Professor Richard Wiseman of the University of Hertfordshire at the Edinburgh International Science Festival (April 2006)

B) **55%**

Eighty-one per cent of women at any one time are waiting for DIY work to be completed – 28% say they have been waiting longer than a year – and, 'as a result of delayed DIY, 55% of couples have argued among themselves'. Odd that the figures should not divulge how many men are waiting for the completion of DIY work.

Source: Direct Line Home Insurance (April 2006)

A) **Estonia**

Over in the Baltic, they carry you over the threshold and just keep going. An Estonian has won the esteemed World Wife-Carrying Championships the last seven years running. As for how the gals reciprocate, we hear the winners are doing some very uplifting things, whereas the losers are just holding out.

Source: CNN

WHAT ARE THE ODDS?

Staggering Statistics

WHICH COUNTRY has attracted the highest percentage of stag and hen party revellers from Britain over the past five years?

A) Czech Republic   B) Holland   C) Spain

Till Death Do They Part

IT'S NO secret that women generally outlive men, although the gap is narrowing. What are the odds a woman will be widowed compared to those of a man becoming a widower?

A) 4/1   B) 6/1   C) 8/1

Text Maniacs

WHAT ARE the odds that a youngster aged 15 or under will dump their boyfriend/girlfriend by text message?

A) Evens   B) 2/1   C) 4/1

LOVE & MARRIAGE

45

C) Spain

The Czech Republic – chiefly Prague – attracted 8% of all British stag and hen parties, while 23% headed for Holland – which almost always meant Amsterdam. The top destination was Spain – principally Barcelona and, somewhat more unexpectedly, Seville. Maybe there are new hen party traditions involving marmalade that haven't yet reached my innocent ears.

Source: Foreign Office; Egg Online; *The Times*; *Daily Mail* (20 April 2006)

A) 4/1

Whether they're loving them to death or working them into an early grave, widows still outnumber widowers 11 million to 2.6 million. Women living longer doesn't quite account for the huge differential, though the stats on the number of older guys with younger wives surely would.

Source: CDC; US Census (2002)

C) 4/1

While 41% of youngsters would still end a relationship face to face, 20% would do so by text (giving a 4/1 chance). It does make me wonder how the remaining 39% do their dumping: e-mail; radio announcement; newspaper ad; carrier pigeon; semaphore?

Source: Ofcom technology survey (May 2006)

WHAT ARE THE ODDS?

Stop Your Sobbing

WHAT PERCENTAGE of men and women have been moved to tears by love songs?

A) 23%   B) 39%   C) 54%

I Can't Stomach You Any More

WHAT PERCENTAGE of men, when asked what cosmetic procedure they would recommend for their other half, plumped for a tummy tuck?

A) 2%   B) 9%   C) 14%

Pray Together . . . Stay Together?

'HOLY MATRIMONY' sounds good at the ceremony, but who's listening? The chance of divorce is lowest among couples who classify their religious beliefs as which of the following?

A) Christian   B) Jewish   C) Atheist

LOVE & MARRIAGE

A) 23% and B) 39%

Almost a quarter of men – 23% – and over a third of women – 39% – say they have welled up whilst listening to a tear-jerking or romantic ballad. I know how they feel. Anything by Whitney Houston or Celine Dion can reduce me to tears within seconds.

Source: Survey by www.ukshallot.com

C) 14%

Breast reduction polled a mere 2% (big surprise!), as did nose jobs and Botox, but 9% of men put their head above the parapet and suggested their nearest and dearest could use some liposuction, while 14% risked disembowelling by advising a tummy tuck. Women were less shy about pointing out their partners' flaws (big surprise, again!): when they were asked the same question, 23% suggested liposuction for their other half. I've had a procedure carried out on me – by my wife, actually – a walletremovaluction. It was painless – for her.

Source: ICM poll for the London Clinic (29 April 2006)

C) Atheist

Whereas 1 in 3 Jewish and Christian couples break their vows by divorcing, apparently only 1 in 5 atheists split up. Maybe they just don't believe in going through the hell of getting divorced.

Source: Barna Research Group (1999)

WHAT ARE THE ODDS?

Yours (Un)faithfully

WHAT PERCENTAGE of men admit to having been unfaithful to their partner

A) 25%   **B)** 32%   **C)** 46%

Staggering Stat

WHAT PERCENTAGE of men say they would consider having one last fling on their stag night?

A) 14%   **B)** 34%   **C)** 74%

D.I.V.O.R.C.E

THE LONDON Borough of Harrow boasts the lowest divorce rate in Britain. What are the odds of a person living there being divorced?

A) 13/1   **B)** 20/1   **C)** 28/1

LOVE & MARRIAGE

ANSWERS . . . .

B) 32%

Of those men who admitted to being unfaithful, 46% said they regretted doing so. But 32% of men had been unfaithful, with 27% of them saying it was because of a poor sex life – the most frequently cited reason.

Source: Survey of over 40,000 people by www.cupidbay.com (6 May 2006)

C) 74%

14% of women quizzed said they had one last fling on a hen night and 34% of women said that they would consider doing so, compared with 74% of men who said they would consider it and 35% who said they had done it. The only fling I woud admit to on a stag night was one which left the underpants of the groom-to-be adorning the local pub sign back in the early seventies. They were still there the last time I checked.

Source: Survey of over 40,000 people by www.cupidbay.com (6 May 2006)

A) 13/1

According to the *Harrow Observer*, 'just 7.3% of the borough's population is divorced – the lowest rate in Britain'. We live in Harrow and when I told my wife about this statistic she refused to believe it and we had such an argument that we may soon be adding to the divorce rate in the borough.

Source: *Harrow Observer* (February 2006)

WHAT ARE THE ODDS?

Till Defeat Do Us Part

WHAT PERCENTAGE of men would switch their allegiance if their football team was underperforming; and what proportion would bale out of their relationship if it was doing likewise?

A) 6%   **B)** 25%   **C)** 52%

What's Yours is Mine and What's Mine is Mine

HOW MANY couples who are getting married or are living together have signed an agreement on how to divide their possessions should they split up?

A) 10%   **B)** 4%   **C)** 1%

Robbed of Their Marriages

WHAT PERCENTAGE of couples whose property is burgled subsequently blame that robbery for the breakdown of their marriage?

A) 9%   **B)** 16%   **C)** 25%

LOVE & MARRIAGE

ANSWERS . . . .

A) 6% and C) 52%, respectively

About 94% of the male respondents to a survey declared that under no circumstances would they ever desert their football team. Compare that with the 52% in the same survey who said they would walk away from a personal relationship which was no longer delivering the goods.

Source: Survey for Duracell (March 2006)

C) 1%

Although 92% of Britons assume they will be able to agree amicably on who gets what, or never even think about it, just 1 in a 100 of those who have bought things together have agreed in advance how to divide them in the future should the need arise.

Source: *Daily Star* (30 March 2006)

A) 9%

A burglary can have an enormous impact on the lives of the victims – 1 in 5 say they subsequently suffered from sleepless nights; 1 in 4 began drinking, smoking or taking drugs to cope with the trauma; a third believed their work suffered; 25% said their relationships with friends altered; 16% said the incident led to increased strain on their relationship; 10% developed sexual problems; and 9% said that the burglary was a contributory factor in the subsequent collapse of their marriage.

Source: *Daily Mail* (17 April 2006)

SEX &
SINNERS

'Women need a reason to have sex. Men need a place.'

Nora Ephron, US novelist and screenwriter

I Think I Fancy Someone Else

WHAT PERCENTAGE of Britons fantasise that they are with someone else while making love to their partner

A) 21%   **B)** 41%   **C)** 61%

Calendar That!

IF YOU'RE in your 40s, you're likely to have sex how many times during the year?

A) 34 Times   **B)** 64 Times   **C)** 84 Times

Granny Gets It On

WHAT IS the chance that a woman over the age of 75 has a sexual partner?

A) 1 in 2   **B)** 1 in 4   **C)** 1 in 10

SEX & SINNERS

55

ANSWERS . . . .

A) 21%

Almost a fifth of those quizzed admitted to being
unfaithful to their partner in their thoughts.

Source: Survey of 3,000 for Durex Big Sex Survey (December 2006)

B) 64 Times

Not very encouraging if you're a 40-something, eh? But
the 18–29 crowd manage only 84 times, and you're
way ahead of your elders, so enjoy it while you can.
After 70, you'll probably be down to about 10 times a
year – no doubt skipping a couple of months to recu-
perate.

Source: Kinsey Institute (2002)

B) 1 in 4

Go, Granny, go! About 25% of women over 75 have
regular sexual partners, while the rest are sticking with
'Not tonight, dear, I've had a heart attack'.

Source: AARP; myhealthyhorizon.com (2003)

Time Zone

HEY, GUYS, **if you live to love, your best odds for 'going for a full half-hour' are with someone from which country?**

A) Brazil **B)** Thailand **C)** United States

Measuring Up

IF THERE'S **anything that really worries guys – other than impotence and pregnancy – it's the size of their penis. The most likely size for an adult man – at attention – is which of the following?**

A) 3–4 Inches **B)** 5–7 Inches **C)** 8–11 Inches

A Roll in the Hay

ACCORDING TO **Dr. Alfred Kinsey's 1950s research, what percentage of farm boys reported having had 'significant' sexual contact with an animal?**

A) 1 out of 100 **B)** 9 out of 100 **C)** 17 out of 100

SEX & SINNERS

57

ANSWERS . . . .

A) Brazil

Another reason to visit Rio! Those torrid Brazilians average 30 minutes per romantic interlude – the longest in the world. Americans come close, at 28 minutes, while Thais are the world's most efficient lovers, at an average of just 10 minutes per sexual encounter.

Source: *Penguin Atlas of Human Sexual Behavior*

B) 5–7 Inches

Yes, you can relax. Most of us aren't endowed like Jake the Peg ('with the extra leg'), but we've got sufficient stature to make a good impression. And walking around with several extra inches dangling between your legs would seem to have its own set of problems. For those of you on the short end of the stick, well … enthusiasm and technique count for a lot … *honestly*.

Source: Kinsey Institute (2002); J. Mackay, *Human Sexual Behavior*

C) 17 out of 100

That's right. 17% of '50s farm boys reported having sexual contact with the livestock – and it wasn't just 'heavy petting'! More recent studies have shown a marked decrease in this form of 'animal husbandry'. In part, we guess, because the media reinforces unrealistic images of animals that are slim and pretty. Or maybe with the decline of small farms there just isn't enough privacy in the barn anymore.

Source: Kinsey Institute (1953)

Pulsating Possibilities

NOT EVERYTHING is **natural, or real, even when it comes to sexual encounters. Of the following, which has a 2 in 5 chance of occurring?**

A) Woman's Faked Orgasm   **B)** Man's Faked Orgasm
C) Woman's Vibrator Use

Gender Benders

LIFE'S A DRAG **for a substantial number of people who would rather be the opposite sex. What's the chance that a male is transsexual?**

A) 1 in 1,200   **B)** 1 in 12,000   **C)** 1 in 120,000

Too Late Now

WHAT PERCENTAGE **of over 65s surveyed said that they wished they had had more sex in their lives?**

A) 57%   **B)** 70%   **C)** 83%

A) **Woman's Faked Orgasm**

About 40% of women are practising fakers, while almost 30% (aged 25–34) own vibrators. Neither of these findings reflects well on their partners' performances! (There were *no* reports of men faking orgasm or gals faking it with their vibrators, oddly enough.) The study was conducted by a condom manufacturer and didn't include lesbian liaisons, by the way.

Source: Durex Annual Sex Survey (2004)

B) **1 in 12,000**

Could *this* be Victoria's Secret? Judging by the numbers, it's a pretty big party of gender dysphoric folk – although fewer than 30% of 'cross-sex' males actually go through the arduous and expensive operations and hormone therapy that turns 'Mike' into 'Michelle'. Of the estimated 7,000–12,000 sex-change operations that have been performed in the US, they're about evenly split, M-T-F and F-T-M.

Source: Dr M. Brown; *Journal of Clinical Endocrinology & Metabolism* (2003)

B) **70%**

57% of the pensioners surveyed regretted not doing more travelling, while just 12% of them wished they had taken education seriously, but seven in ten were concerned that they had missed out on the pleasures of the flesh.

Source: UKTV Gold Survey of 1,500 pensioners (October 2006)

WHAT ARE THE ODDS?

Bound for Glory

IT TAKES more to get some people going than others. What's the chance that a guy is into bondage?

A) 3 in 100   **B)** 7 in 100   **C)** 11 in 100

Blatant or Latent?

WHAT ARE the chances that an American woman who contracts chlamydia will be totally symptom-free?

A) 1 in 4   **B)** 2 in 4   **C)** 3 in 4

Self-Contained

GREEK MYTHOLOGY tells of Hermaphroditus, a young man whose body was fused with his female lover by the gods. What is the chance of someone being born a hermaphrodite – with both male and female sex organs?

A) 1 in 125,000   **B)** 1 in 250,000   **C)** 1 in 375,000

SEX & SINNERS

61

C) **11 in 100**

If you're a guy with this kink in your kit, you probably won't have trouble finding a playmate – or *two* – to string along, because 17 in every 100 women share your passion.

Source: Kinsey Institute (2002)

C) **3 in 4**

What you don't know *can* hurt you. Three-quarters of female chlamydia sufferers and 50% of men with the disease have no discernible symptoms at all. And that's particularly scary because, untreated, chlamydia can cause irreversible infertility by scarring of the Fallopian tubes – a condition affecting an estimated 100,000 women a year in the US.

Source: D. Yancy, *STDs: What You Don't Know Can Hurt You*; NIAID (2004)

B) **1 in 250,000**

There are an estimated 1,100 intersexuals (hermaphrodites) in the US. For anyone into group sex, this may seem like a free pass, but it's not nearly as much fun – or as funny – as it sounds. Plus, you have to be really, really careful not to get pregnant when you masturbate!

Source: www.nih.gov

WHAT ARE THE ODDS?

Lip Service

WHAT ARE the odds that teen girls don't consider oral sex as having sex at all?

A) 38%   **B)** 58%   **C)** 78%

Getting Enough

WHAT PERCENTAGE of people have sex 'more than 20 times' in an average month?

A) 2%   **B)** 7%   **C)** 12%

Breast of the Bunch

OFFERED A choice including 'breasts', 'backsides', 'face' and 'personality' as the feature attracting them most to women, what were the odds of a man opting for 'personality'?

A) 4/1   **B)** 8/1   **C)** 12/1

SEX & SINNERS

63

ANSWERS ....

A) **38%**

Are these girls just paying 'lip service' to the idea of virginity? Maybe. But at least 47% of teen boys agree. Of course, 80% of the oral sex was girl-on-guy, so the guys certainly have a vested interest in keeping the illusion alive.

Source: *People* magazine and the *Today* show (2005)

B) **7%**

In a December 2005 poll, 18% answered that they never had sex; 11% reckoned on just twice a month; 22% 6–10 times. And then there was that 7% who somehow summoned the energy to fill in the form.

Source: *Observer*

B) **8/1**

Breasts and backsides were the most likely choices, with 1 in 6 respondents choosing each of them. Personality is over-rated – how many winners of the annual BBC TV Sports Personality of the Year award ever exhibit any signs of having one?

Source: *Mail on Sunday* (11 December 2005)

Choc Full of Sex

WHAT PERCENTAGE of British people surveyed
believed that chocolate boosted their sex life?

A) 2%   **B)** 4%   **C)** 5%

Bent Out of Shape

WHEN A guy's 'Mr Happy' looks more like something a plumber would call a 'bad connection',
it's usually Peyronie's Disease. What's the
chance this condition will mangle the member
of someone you know?

A) 1 in 100   **B)** 1 in 1,000   **C)** 1 in 1,000,000

Toy Time

WHAT PERCENTAGE of British women aged 18 to
50 own a sex toy?

A) 20%   **B)** 50%   **C)** 80%

SEX & SINNERS

65

ANSWERS . . . .

B) 47%

The French were the biggest believers in the libido-enhancing properties of chocolate, while only 2% of Germans and 4% of Britons bought into the idea.

Source: Survey of 3,016 people by Ipsos for Barry Callebaut (2007)

C) 1 in 1,000,000

Sounds rare, but there's a small army of 40 to 60-year old guys out there in loose fitting boxers hoping to go undetected when they get an erection. The deformity was discovered by French sugeon Francois de la Peyronie in 1743. There are surgical and nonsugical treatments but with something like this, you certainly don't want to take any shortcuts.

Source: www.urologychannel.com

C) 80%

According to a 2006 survey four-fifths of British women in that age group now own a sex toy. However I don't think men were classified as 'sex toys'.

Source: Ann Summers

Dream Lovers

WHAT ARE the odds that when a man or woman drifts off to sleep he or she will dream about sex?

A) 4/1   **B)** 8/1   **C)** 12/1

Sexy Scenes

WHEN 120,000 movie-goers were asked to name their sexiest scene in a movie, what came out on top?

A) A gay kiss in *Brokeback Mountain*   **B)** George Clooney locking J-Lo in the boot in *Out of Sight*
C) The boss spanking the eponymous 'Secretary'

Loving Eyes

WHAT PERCENTAGE of Britons look at pornography at least once a day?

A) 30%   B) 24%   C) 7%

SEX & SINNERS

C) 12/1

In the 1960s when the subject was last investigated, women claimed just half as many sex dreams as men. New research by Canadian psychology professor Antonio Zadra, in which those studied kept 'dream diaries', showed that there was a 12/1 chance (8%) of both males and females dreaming about sex.

Source: Motreal University (June 2007)

C) The Boss Spanking the Eponymous 'Secretary'

James Spader and Maggie Gyllenhaal spanked the opposition, thrashing Heath Ledger and Jake Gyllenhaal's (what is it with these Gyllenhaals?) snog and George and J-Lo's in-car action. How could anything beat that?

Source: www.lovefilm.com 2006 survey

B) 24%

British men are apparently the most voracious viewers of porn in Europe, with 24% peeping at it on a daily basis, compared with 15% of Germans, 9% of French men and 7% of Italian stallions. Top of the world chart were the Brazilians, with 30% indulging daily.

Source: *Men's Health Magazine* survey of 40,000 men in 20 countries (August 2006)

Breast of Both Worlds?

WHAT ARE the odds that a woman's breasts will be exactly the same shape and size?

A) 10/1   B) 50/1   C) 100/1

Stand and Deliver?

WHAT PERCENTAGE of British women in a poll admitted to having had a one-night stand?

A) 33%   **B)** 12%   **C)** 10%

Porn to be Wild

WHICH TOWN is the 'porn capital of Britain'?

A) Bournemouth   **B)** Hull   **C)** London

SEX & SINNERS

69

ANSWERS . . . .

C) 100/1

In a study involving the examination of the breasts of 504 women, researchers at the University of Liverpool discovered that only around 1% of them had a perfectly symmetrical pair.

Source: *Guardian* (20 March 2006)

C) 10%

Of course, admitting to it – or claiming it – is not the same as actually doing it, but in a survey by psychologists, 90% of women said they thought casual sex was wrong, while 10% admitted to at least one one-night stand.

Source: Sheffield University (March 2006)

B) Hull

The lowest percentage of total porn DVD rentals among twelve cities recorded by the UK's largest online videostore was in Bournemouth, with just 2.5%. London accounted for 6.6% of porn rentals, taking fifth place in the chart. Hull, the outright winner, was responsible for 20%, accounting for twice as many as second-place Cardiff.

Source: www.lovefilm.com (April 2006)

Lust for Words

WHAT PERCENTAGE of UK men believe that 'sex is important'?

A) 30%   **B)** 45%   **C)** 75%

French Polishing

WHAT ARE the odds that a woman will find housework more satisfying than sex?

A) 2/1   **B)** 4/1   **C)** 8/1

Mixing Business with Pleasure

WHAT PERCENTAGE of those questioned for a 2005 sex survey claimed to have had sex at work?

A) 15%   **B)** 55%   **C)** 69%

SEX & SINNERS

ANSWERS . . . .

B) 45%

The survey took in 27,500 men and women from 29
countries, with the ladies of Israel giving the highest
'yes' vote to the question – 55% of them agreed it was
important, compared with just 30% of UK women.
While that probably means that a lot of British women
are being pestered by their menfolk, they should just
be glad they don't live in Brazil, where 75% of the men
voted in favour of the, er, motion.

Source: Archives of Sexual Behaviour (April 2006)

A) 2/1

In a poll of 2,000 women, 64% said that housework
made them happy (of the 8% who have a cleaner, 57%
tidy up before she arrives!). But the most eye-catching
result was the admission by 33% that 'cleaning gives
them more satisfaction than sex'.

Source: 'Cleanaholics', Discovery Home & Health Channel (April 2006)

A) 15%

Fifty per cent of British workers claim that they never
even get to take a lunch break, which probably means
they are not among the 15% who have had sex at
work. But what about people working in the sex trade?
Were they asked whether they ever worked during sex?

Source: Durex Global Sex Survey (2005)

KEEP IT IN THE FAMILY

'Like all the best families we have our share of eccentricities, of impetuous and wayward youngsters and of family disagreements.'

HRH Elizabeth II

Happy Birthdays

HOW MANY **people do you need in a room to make it an even money chance that at least two of them will have the same birthday (excluding any born on 29 February)?**

A) 23   **B)** 183   **C)** 365

Many Happy Returns, and Returns, and Returns

A MOTHER **whose birthday is 17 June, married to a husband whose birthday is also 17 June, gives birth to their first baby on 17 June. What are the odds of the mother doing that?**

A) 364/1   **B)** 132,496/1   **C)** Over 1,000,000/1

Quad Odds

WHAT ARE **the odds of a mother giving birth to quads?**

A) 16,000,000/1   **B)** 32,000,000/1   **C)** 64,000,000/1

ANSWERS . . . .

A) 23

Give yourself a special birthday present if you opted for the lowest figure. Don't believe it? Try it the next time there are 23 people at one of your parties.

Source: Rob Eastaway and Jeremy Wyndham, *Why Do Buses Come in Threes?* (Robson Books, 1998)

A) 364/1

The baby had to be born on one date in the year. As there are 365 dates in the year, of which 17 June is one, the odds that the baby – unless induced – would be born on that date are 364/1.

C) 64,000,000/1

Julie Carles, from Bedford, was that one in 64 million in March 2006. Although Julie, 37, had considered undergoing fertility treatment, she finally conceived naturally after years of trying. Holly, Ellie, Georgina and Jessica duly arrived. Only 60 other sets of quadruplets have been born worldwide since 1930 without the aid of fertility treatment.

Source: *Daily Mail* (3 April 2006)

Kids' Stuff

WHAT PERCENTAGE of parents resent having had their children once they realise how much they cost?

A) 4% **B)** 14% **C)** 44%

Relatively at Home

WHAT PERCENTAGE of British men aged between 25 and 29 are still living with their parents?

A) 18% **B)** 23% **C)** 36%

Baby Talk

WHAT ARE the odds that an English girl aged under 18 will be a mother?

A) 8/1 **B)** 12/1 **C)** 16/1

KEEP IT IN THE FAMILY

A) 4%

Although children become increasingly expensive (and often less grateful) as they grow up – until, by the age of 16, they are costing £64 each week – only 1 in every 25 parents said they regretted having them because of the cost.

Source: *Guardian* (16 February 2006)

B) 23%

Women in the same age group are much more keen to fly the nest, with only 11% of them sticking it out with Mum and Dad.

Source: *Guardian* (21 February 2006)

C) 16/1

England is top of Europe's teen pregnancy league table, with 6% of English girls giving birth before they are (legally) allowed to drink.

Source: *News of the World* (12 March 2006)

Daddy's Girl?

WHAT PERCENTAGE of British daughters are given a financial helping hand by their parents to get on the property ladder?

A) 27%   **B)** 44%   **C)** 61%

Outing Family Outings

WHAT ARE the odds that a family has been turned away from a restaurant because they had a child with them?

A) 85%   **B)** 34%   **C)** 7%

Keeping Mum

WHAT PERCENTAGE of British women over 50 believe their mothers are interfering old biddies?

A) 9%   **B)** 6%   **C)** 4%

KEEP IT IN THE FAMILY

79

ANSWERS . . . .

C) 61%

A study showed that 44% of sons get some cash for their first home from their parents, with their folks shelling out an average of £4,200 for the purpose. The girls do rather better. Parents provide almost twice as much financial assistance to their daughters, with the average first-time female buyer pocketing some £7,240, and 61% of all daughters receiving some help from Mummy and Daddy.

Source: Co-operative Bank (March 2006)

B) 34%

Seven per cent reported that they had been told to stop breastfeeding while on a family outing; 85% believe that restaurants view children as a nuisance and 34% have actually been turned away from such establishments for having the kids in tow.

Source: Baby Friendly Britain Campaign survey of 3000 mothers, *Mother & Baby Magazine* (July 2006)

A) 9%

In a survey ironically released to coincide with Mothering Sunday in 2006, almost 1 in 10 of the over 50s thought that their mother 'interferes in my life'. Only 1 in 20 under 30s felt the same way/I call my mother-in-law 'old Biddy'. She thinks I'm joking.

Source: YouGov for the Social Issues Research Centre

IVF IVF

WHAT ARE the odds that fertility treatment will produce twins?

A) 4/1   **B)** 9/1   **C)** 200/1

A Nappy Arrangement

WHAT ARE the odds that the male in a relationship will be the first to change a new baby's nappy?

A) 7/2   **B)** 10/1   **C)** 100/1

Who'd Have 'Em?

WHAT PERCENTAGE of British people do not want kids?

A) 16%   **B)** 23%   **C)** 30%

KEEP IT IN THE FAMILY

A) 4/1

About 1% of all British births are IVF babies, and about 20% of them are twins; 0.5% are triplets. The highest success rate for IVF treatment is for women under 35, for whom it is 27.6%.

Source *The Times* (29 March 2006)

A) 7/2

A substantial 11% of women reckoned that 'the father would be mainly responsible' for their baby during its first year, although 96% accepted responsibility for the night-time feeds (which is fortunate, as they have the right equipment). 78% of women said that they had to carry out the first nappy change.

Source: Survey for John Lewis (April 2006)

B) 23%

Men are much less broody than women, with 30% of them preferring to remain childless, against just 16% of women who were questioned. That gives a total of 23% who would rather do without kids, with 37% of them saying they feel that way because they are unwilling to compromise their lifestyle.

Source: Skipton Building Society (April 2006)

You Must Be Kidding

WHAT PERCENTAGE of women said they would have preferred no one, or someone other than their partner to have been present when they gave birth?

A) 2%   **B)** 38%   **C)** 74%

Bedtime? What's That?

WHAT PERCENTAGE of parents want schools to advise them about their children's bedtimes?

A) 9%   **B)** 22%   **C)** 40%

IKEAn't Believe It!

WHAT PERCENTAGE of Europeans are now conceived on IKEA beds?

A) 5%   **B)** 10%   **C)** 20%

KEEP IT IN THE FAMILY

83

B) 38%

A survey of 1,400 parents found that 1 in 7 women believe there is 'nothing much' that husbands/partners can do at a birth, and 40% of fathers agree, admitting that they felt 'fairly useless' throughout the whole process. Over 15% of them believe that they 'just get in the way' in the delivery room.

Source: Royal College of Midwives (May 2006)

C) 40%

In a poll of 500 parents of 5–16-year-olds, 40% couldn't work out for themselves what time to send the little darlings to bed. The survey showed that schools are clearly shirking their responsibilities in this regard, as only 9% of them were doling out advice. Coming soon – school instruction on what time children should tie their shoelaces each morning!

Source: *Times Educational Supplement* (May 2006)

B) 10%

It surely won't be long before flat-pack babies are on the shelves. But until that day arrives, it seems fans of the Swedish mega-conglomerate will have to continue to do it themselves. Presumably, those who managed to conceive on the beds were among the lucky ones who received all the nuts, bolts and, er, screws they needed when they bought their furniture.

Source: *The Indypedia* 2006

ANIMAL MAGIC

'People are not going to care about animal conservation unless they think that animals are worthwhile.'

David Attenborough

Nearer My Dog to Thee

WHAT PROPORTION of UK dog owners give their deceased pooch a special burial or cremation service?

A) 2 in 5   **B)** 2 in 10   **C)** 2 in 20

Breeding Awful

WHAT PERCENTAGE of dogs stolen in Britain are taken for breeding purposes?

A) 20%   **B)** 50%   **C)** 95%

Pussy or Pooch?

WHAT PERCENTAGE of British household pets are cats?

A) 19.9%   **B)** 24.4%   **C)** 27.8%

ANIMAL MAGIC

A) 2 in 5

Yes, 40% of dog owners now provide a funeral service
for their conked-out canines, with 75% of those believ-
ing this to be as important as a family funeral.

Source: Direct Line Pet Insurance (February 2006)

C) 95%

There is apparently an epidemic of lost and stolen dogs
in Britain, with www.doglost.com being alerted to 200
lost dogs every month. Ninety-five per cent of stolen
dogs are pedigree bitches that have been taken to be
used for breeding,' reported the *Sunday Express*, adding,
'the most popular breeds for dognappers are Labradors,
Lurchers, Spaniels and Jack Russell terriers.'

Source: *Daily Express* (19 February 2006)

B) 24.4%

In 2003, 52.7% of UK households owned a pet.
Goldfish were the third most popular, with 8.6% of
pet-owning households having at least one. Dogs came
next, making up 20.9% of the total, meaning that for
once they had to acknowledge the pre-eminence of
cats.

Source: *Guardian*

Catastrophe?

AFTER SPOTTING a mysterious big cat in the English countryside, what are the odds that the observer would describe it as a 'panther-like black cat'?

A) 4/6   **B)** 6/4   **C)** 6/1

How Great Is That Tit?

WHAT ARE the odds that your garden will get a visit from a great tit?

A) 8/11   **B)** 11/8   **C)** 11/4

Shark Shocker

WHAT ARE the odds that your death will be the result of a shark attack?

A) 685,000/1   **B)** 3,500,000/1   **C)** 300,000,000/1

ANIMAL MAGIC

89

A) 4/6

There were 2,123 sightings of 'big cats' between January and July 2005, according to the British Big Cats Society – allegedly including tigers, pumas and lynxes. How many of them were a potential threat to grazing sheep is another matter, as the Society revealed that one picture of a 'panther' that was published by two tabloid newspapers was actually a life-size cuddly toy. Nevertheless, 60% of sightings described 'panther-like black cats'; 32% were said to be 'brown, puma-like creatures'; and 6% were 'lynx-like'.

Source: British Big Cats Society (March 2006)

A) 8/11

Blue tits were spotted in 84.4% of the 270,000 gardens contributing to the RSPB Big Garden Birdwatch survey, whose results were announced in March 2006. Great tits were more rare, being reported in just 57.1% of gardens. The most widespread bird was the blackbird, in evidence in 94.7% of gardens.

C) 300,000,000/1

Dying of fright while watching *Jaws* doesn't count, but calculations revealed a 300,000,000/1 chance of being a victim of one of the 40 or so fatal shark attacks each year; this compares with 3,500,000/1 that you will go out via a snakebite (animal, not alcoholic) and 685,000/1 that you will drown in the bath.

Source: *Daily Mirror* (1 August 2006)

Dog's Dinner

WHAT PERCENTAGE of British vets have had to treat a dog or a cat because of the after-effects of it being fed food intended for human consumption?

A) 6%   **B)** 36%   **C)** 87%

What's Up, Hen?

WHAT ARE the odds that a hen will turn into a cockerel?

A) 1,000/1   **B)** 10,000/1   **C)** 100,000/1

Heavy Petting

WHAT PERCENTAGE of women who own pets say their animal is 'more important than any man'?

A) 50%   **B)** 75%   **C)** 100%

ANIMAL MAGIC

C) 87%

And apparently more of these cases are admitted into vets' surgeries every year. Usually the problem arises because Rex or Fluffy has been fed confectionery and/or chocolate, which could kill them as it contains substances called methylxanthines.

Source: Halifax Pet Insurance (March 2006)

B) 10,000/1

Freaky the hen startled owner Jo Richards of Bristol by turning into a cockerel after *ten years* as a hen. 'She' stopped laying eggs and began crowing at dawn. Victoria Roberts, of the Poultry Club of Great Britain, explained: 'It's very, very rare – about a one in ten thousand event. Only one ovary normally functions in a chicken, the left one. If that gets damaged then the other one kicks into life – but the jump in testosterone that causes can change it into a testis. That, in turn, causes a flood of hormones which spark changes in the way the chicken looks, with the growth of new plumage, a wattle and comb. Sometimes they crow, but they cannot reproduce.' So poor old Freaky is something of a hender-bender, you might say.

Source: *Daily Express* (19 April 2006)

B) 75%

Half of the women polled answered that they would not commit to any guy who did not like their pet. A startling 10% claimed that their pet had actually tried to oust their man from the relationship. 'There are three of us in this relationship – us two and *him*,' said Polly the parrot!

Source: National Pet Week poll (April 2006)

LITTLE
BRITAIN

'The British nation is unique in this respect. They are the only people who like to be told how bad things are, who like to be told the worst.'

Winston Churchill

ANSWERS ➤

God Save the Queen

WHAT PERCENTAGE of Britons in the 1960s 'thought Her Majesty had been hand-picked by God'?

A) 4%   **B)** 17%   **C)** 30%

Auld Lang What?

WHAT ARE the odds that a British New Year reveller will be able to sing the first verse of Auld Lang Syne in full?

A) 7/4   **B)** 7/2   **C)** 7/1

Home Surfing

HOW LONG do British internet users spend online on an average day?

A) 164 minutes   **B)** 114 minutes   **C)** 94 minutes

LITTLE BRITAIN

95

C) 30%

According to a poll conducted in 1964, almost a third of Britons reckoned the Queen had every right to call herself 'Defender of the Faith'. Mind you, she's not held in quite such high esteem these days. A survey in 2000 suggested that only 44% believed that the country would be worse off without the monarchy. And the following year a Mori poll revealed that only 1 in 10 'considered the royal family good value for money'. Helen Mirren is a great fan, though!

Source: *Guardian* (11 April 2006)

B) 7/2

Researchers found that Rabbie Burns' lyrics defeated 22% of all Brits, with many of the others confessing that they hummed 'sort of Scottish noises' to cover their ignorance late at night on 31 December.

Source: *Guardian* (28 December 2006)

A) 164 minutes

A 2006 survey of 1,000 adults aged between 16 and 64 found that men clocked up an average of 172 minutes a day, compared to women's 156 minutes – giving an average online of 164 minutes per day. That means surfing has now surpassed TV-watching (148 minutes) as the chief pastime in British homes each day.

Source: Google

Bog Standard

IN LONDON there is a public convenience for every how many people?

A) 6,000   **B)** 12,000   **C)** 18,000

I Resolve to Have No Resolve

AFTER THREE days of 2006, what proportion of people who had made a New Year's resolution had already given it up?

A) 1 in 4   **B)** 2 in 4   **C)** 3 in 4

Sunny Side Up

WHAT PERCENTAGE of Britons contemplating emigrating said that the main reason was Britain's weather?

A) 24%   **B)** 32%   **C)** 37%

LITTLE BRITAIN

97

C) 18,000

In 2000 there were 700 public conveniences for London's 7 million inhabitants. That was hardly generous, but by 2006 there was a wee bit more to worry about because the number had fallen to 400. And don't get caught short on the Tube: fewer than 90 of London Underground's 255 stations have lavatories.

Source: London Assembly Health and Public Services Committee

A) 1 in 4

But before you other three start patting yourselves on the back, 73% of Brits had reportedly given up by mid-February. And a National Savings and Investments survey predicted that only 8% of resolutions would survive the whole year.

Source: *News of the World* (19 February 2006)

B) 32%

Almost a quarter, 24%, said they wanted to go because Britain has become too expensive; and the greatest number, 37%, said they were looking for a better quality of life, with 32% claiming they were chasing climate contentment.

Source: Institute of Public Policy Research (December 2006)

That's News to Me

WHAT PROPORTION of people say that their main source of information is television?

A) 20%   **B)** 45%   **C)** 73%

Must-Watch TV

WHICH MAJOR event gathered the largest ever UK TV viewing figures?

A) Funeral of Princess Diana (1997)   **B)** Royal Family Documentary (1969)   **C)** World Cup Final (1966)

Green Around the Gills

WHAT PERCENTAGE of people declared that they were fed up with hearing about ethical and environmental issues?

A) 28%   **B)** 35%   **C)** 63%

LITTLE BRITAIN

C) 73%

A survey for Ofcom discovered that 10% of Brits keep up to date via their radio, while 13% rely on the papers, but 73% tune in to learn what's going on in the world. Presumably the missing 4% rely on the internet, or perhaps town criers.

Source: *Guardian* (13 March 2006)

C) World Cup Final

30.69 million watched the royal family documentary at the end of the sixties; and 32.10 million of the 'nation united in grief' saw Diana's final send-off (almost 4 million more than watched her wedding, by the way). But England's 4–2 win over Germany in 1966 has never been surpassed, with 32.30 million tuning in (and not one of them was Scottish, apparently).

Source: *Guardian* (March 2006)

A) 28%

Although 28% said that they were fed up with the whole thing, 35% asked 'What's the point?' and a hefty 63% said they believed that it is 'all about companies making themselves look good'.

Source: Survey of 2,052 people by Mintel (February 2007)

Hello? Is It Good Nudes?

WHAT ARE the odds that an individual will have made a phone call in the nude?

A) 2/1   **B)** 8/1   **C)** 33/1

Driving Ambition

WHAT PERCENTAGE of adult Britons hold a valid driving licence?

A) 71%   **B)** 60%   **C)** 48%

Testing Times

WHAT PERCENTAGE of British driving tests result in a pass?

A) 63%   **B)** 53%   **C)** 43%

LITTLE BRITAIN

A) 2/1

According to a Post Office survey, nearly a third of Britons are just too desperate to talk to bother getting dressed first.

Source: *Sun* (24 March 2006)

A) 71%

That means there are 32.1 million licence holders in Great Britain ... and presumably another 14 million or so adults who like to be chauffeured around.

Source: *UK 2005*

C) 43%

In 1992 half of all driving tests resulted in a pass, but clearly the examiners are getting more strict, which makes you wonder why there are still so many idiots on the road.

Source: *UK 2005*

Driving You Mad

HOW MUCH was the first British driver's licence?

A) A quid   **B)** 5 bob   **C)** Half a crown

Video Killed the Radio Star

AT THEIR peak in 1998, how many British homes possessed a videocassette recorder?

A) 93%   **B)** 71%   **C)** 44%

Boozy Brits

WHAT IS the average consumption of beer for a Briton every time he or she visits a bar or restaurant?

A) 6.3 Pints   **B)** 4.1 Pints   **C)** 2.2 Pints

LITTLE BRITAIN

103

ANSWERS . . . .

B) 5 bob

The Motor Car Act of 1903 required all motor vehicles in the UK to be registered and all drivers to be licensed annually. The registration cost a quid and the licence 5 bob (25p in today's money). As a pound back then could buy you a three-bed semi and a new suit, and still leave you change for a bag of chips (or so your great-granddad would tell you), it's safe to say that motoring used to be a preserve of the rich.

A) 93%

But by April 2006, the British Video Association declared, 'Last year 95 DVDs were sold for every five VHS tapes.' Of course, this is yet another example of perfectly serviceable equipment being replaced by something else that does precisely the same thing – like 78s being replaced by 45s, by eight tracks, by cassettes, by CDs, by mini-discs ...

Source: *Daily Mail* (31 March 2006)

C) 2.2 Pints

That makes Britons Europe's top beer boozers when they go out. Germans and Spaniards downed an average of 1.9 pints of beer or lager per visit, while the Swedes were the most abstemious (at least where beer is concerned – the survey didn't ask about vodka!) at 1.5 pints. Given the price of a pint in Stockholm, it's hardly surprising that they keep a tight rein on their tippling.

Source: *Financial Times* (8 April 2006)

Working on the Middle

WHAT PERCENTAGE of the British population
believe themselves to be 'middle class'?

A) 30%   **B)** 43%   **C)** 53%

Everybody Needs Good Neighbours

WHAT PERCENTAGE of people believe their neighbours to be entirely trustworthy?

A) 7%   **B)** 14%   **C)** 78%

Not a Ghost of a Chance

WHAT PERCENTAGE of the British public believe
they have seen a ghost?

A) 12%   **B)** 26%   **C)** 68%

LITTLE BRITAIN

B) 43%

Class-conscious Brits were asked how they saw themselves. The number opting for 'working class' has declined from 65% in 1966 to a current 53%, while those of a 'middle-class' persuasion rose from 30% to 43%. Of those polled, just 3% had no idea what class they were, which hardly indicates that we are now living in 'classless Britain', no matter what the politicians might say. Incidentally, 2.67 million of those describing themselves as 'working class' are among the richest 20% in the land.

Source: Liverpool Victoria (May 2006)

A) 7%

Seventy-eight per cent of over-65s like to chat to their neighbours at least once a week, while just 14% of the same age group have no contact with them. However, only 7% of all age groups think the people living next door can be fully trusted, with a June 2006 survey for Cornhill Insurance showing that 15% actively distrust their neighbours.

Source: *The Indypedia* 2006

A) 12%

A spooky 68% of Britons say they believe in ghosts, but only 12% reckon they have actually seen one. Twenty-six per cent of those quizzed believe in UFOs, while 4% have faith that the Monster is lurking somewhere in Loch Ness.

Source: *Choices* (October 2005)

WHAT ARE THE ODDS?

Clacton, Here We Come!

WHAT PERCENTAGE **of holidays taken by Brits are in the UK?**

A) 33%   **B)** 44%   **C)** 55%

Yanks a Lot

WHAT PERCENTAGE **of tourists visiting the UK are American?**

A) 13%   **B)** 18%   **C)** 26%

Long to Reign Over Us?

WHAT PERCENTAGE **of her subjects believe that the Queen should remain on the throne until she dies, rather than abdicate?**

A) 29%   **B)** 58%   **C)** 87%

LITTLE BRITAIN

107

ANSWERS . . . .

C) 55%

Package holidays account for almost a third of our
hols, with Spain, Greece and Turkey the most popular
destinations, but of 66.3 million holidays taken during
2005 – up from 59.4 million in 2004 – 55% were taken
in the UK. Of those going abroad, 7% took three or
more holidays during the year.

Source: Thomas Cook (May 2006)

A) 13%

Just 18% of adult Americans have a valid passport,
according to the US government, but they still form
the largest group of visitors to the UK. That's largest in
numbers, although they are also probably the largest in
… well, let's not go there – I don't want to upset the
special relationship we have with our Yankee friends.

Source: www.visitbritain.co.uk (May 2006)

B) 58%

Almost 50% of British people think William should
succeed the Queen rather than his old man and less
than half think Charles will be a decent monarch
should he become King. A 58% majority seem happy
for Her Maj to hang around until she pegs it rather
than step down to give her frustrated son a go at the
big job. Coincidentally (or not) 58% is also the exact
figure who do not wish to see Camilla become Queen.

Source: *Mail on Sunday* (23 April 2006)

MONEY MATTERS

'The amount of financial and imaginative energy that's put into mediocrity is just amazing, which I find to be fundamentally offensive as a human being.'

William Hurt

Amazonian Natives

HOW MUCH does the average internet user spend on online shopping per year?

A) £266   **B)** £446   **C)** £626

Put Me Down for a Fiver

WHAT PERCENTAGE of Britons donated £5 or more to charity during 2005?

A) 64%   **B)** 36%   **C)** 25%

Now *That's* a Bargain

WHAT PERCENTAGE of items on sale in the four big supermarkets are 'loss leaders' (being sold to you for less than the supermarket itself paid for them)?

A) 3%   **B)** 2%   **C)** 1%

MONEY MATTERS

111

ANSWERS . . . .

B) £446

A TNS survey for Google revealed that average internet users are now buying everything from groceries to clothes to holidays to cars online.

Source: *Daily Mail* (8 March 2006)

A) 64%

Mintel carried out research which showed that the most generous age group for charitable donations were those presumably least able to afford them – pensioners – with three-quarters of those aged 65 or older donating a fiver or more during 2005. The figure for the population as a whole was significantly lower, and just 44% of 15–24-year-olds managed to spare a fiver. However, 85% of all Britons gave something, and 30% coughed up £100 or more.

Source: Charity Commission

A) 3%

Announcing an inquiry into the dominance of the big four supermarkets –Tesco, Asda, Sainsbury's and Morrison's – the Office of Fair Trading identified 2,708 products being sold below cost price, amounting to 3% of all items. But a whopping 7% of drinks were sold at less than cost price.

Source: *Guardian* (10 March 2006)

See It, Like It, Buy It

WHAT PERCENTAGE of house hunters snap up the property they fancy after seeing it just once?

A) 25%   **B)** 35%   **C)** 45%

Handbag Ladies

WHAT IS the value of the average British handbag and its contents?

A) £377   **B)** £477   **C)** £577

Debt's the Way to Do It

WHAT PERCENTAGE of British 20–29-year-olds have one or more overdrawn accounts in their name?

A) 12%   **B)** 24%   **C)** 36%

MONEY MATTERS

113

B) 35%

According to a survey for Scottish Widows Bank, 35% of prospective property purchasers make up their minds at the first viewing. If you watch Phil and Kirstie's *Location, Location, Location* regularly, though, you'll see couples making their minds up on first viewing – only to change them on the second!

Source: *Daily Mail* (17 March 2006)

C) £577

Handbag sales have risen by almost 150% in the last five years, with women now spending £350 million on them each year. But while they are not cheap, it's what's inside them – make-up, phone, house keys, sunglasses, diary, iPod – that really makes them so pricey to replace.

Source: *Daily Mail* (17 March 2006)

B) 24%

The least debt-burdened age group is the over-70s, with just 1% of them having overdrafts – although that could just be because the banks refuse to grant them one! Unsurprisingly, the 20–29-year-olds are the most indebted sector of society (at least in terms of overdrafts).

Source: Financial Services Authority (March 2006)

WHAT ARE THE ODDS?

Working Retirement

WHAT PERCENTAGE of pensioners have to return to work for 14 or more hours a week to make ends meet?

A) 1%   **B)** 10%   **C)** 50%

Changing Rooms

WHAT PERCENTAGE of the cost of running a home goes on alterations and improvements?

A) 13%   **B)** 29%   **C)** 59%

A Place in the Sun

WHAT PERCENTAGE of Britons aged 45–54 are planning to spend their tax-free pension fund lump sum on buying a property abroad?

A) 13%   **B)** 17%   **C)** 35%

MONEY MATTERS

115

B) 10%

One in ten of the retired people surveyed by GE Life said that they worked an average of 14 hours a week in part-time employment. That's the Father Christmas shortages covered then.

Source: *Times* Online (March 2006)

A) 13%

Mortgage repayments account for some 59% of the £10,000-plus costs of running an average home, with 13% (that's over a grand a year!) going on so-called improvements, often sparked by ideas seen on TV makeover programmes. Sarah Beany has a lot to answer for.

Source: Sainsbury's Bank (April 2006)

B) 17%

Of over 1,000 people quizzed, 20% plan to use the money to set their children up on the property ladder; 13% clearly think they've already done more than enough for the kids and are planning to buy a second home for themselves in Britain; 33% will pay off their existing mortgage. The greatest number, 35%, plan to travel with the cash. Seventeen per cent want to buy a posh foreign home somewhere they can get away from it all and live surrounded by thousands of others who have had the same idea.

Source: Lloyds TSB Private Banking (April 2006)

Brass in Pocket

WHAT PERCENTAGE of youngsters who receive pocket money regularly save some of it?

A) 49%   **B)** 59%   **C)** 69%

Egged On

WHEN STOPPED randomly in the street, what percentage of people were prepared to divulge confidential information which could make them victims of identity theft?

A) 80%   **B)** 86%   **C)** 90%

All By Myself

WHAT PERCENTAGE of the *Sunday Times* Rich List are 'self-made' millionaires?

A) 7.6%   **B)** 41.9%   **C)** 76.7%

MONEY MATTERS

117

ANSWERS . . . .

A) 49%

What a sensible set of little ones we've raised, although the survey didn't reveal what they then blew their savings on when they'd amassed enough – don't suppose they spend it on *Beano* or *Bunty* and a few gobstoppers these days. Average pocket money has recently declined from £8.37 to £8.20 per week – although girls receive 12% more than boys – but almost half still manage to save on a weekly basis.

Source: Halifax (April 2006)

C) 90%

Virtually *all* personal information can be used in some way by fraudsters, so it's best not to hand out any whatsoever to some bloke with a clipboard. One bogus survey stopped 300 people and offered them the chance of winning a £60 Easter egg in a draw. Eighty per cent of those quizzed handed over their date of birth; the same percentage revealed their mother's maiden name; 86% were happy to divulge their pet's name. All of these are standard security questions asked by banks or might well have been used as internet passwords.

Source: Infosecurity Europe (April 2006)

C) 76.7%

Silver spoons are all well and good, but you are three times as likely to get into the *really* big league if you earn your money yourself. Mummy and Daddy were responsible for the inherited wealth of just 23.3% of the list, leaving 76.7% who have accumulated the loot by the sweat of their own brows. Chart-topping steel magnate Lakshmi Mittal, 55, was worth the small matter of £14.88 billion. Yeah, but is he happy?

Source: *Sunday Times* Rich List (2006)

FOOD FOR THOUGHT & DRINK FOR PLEASURE

'The golden rule of reading a menu is: if you can't pronounce it, you can't afford it.'

The late comic writer, Frank Muir

Cheesed Off

WHAT PERCENTAGE of Welsh children asked
where cheese came from were unaware that it
had anything to do with cows or sheep?

A) 3%   **B)** 11%   **C)** 14%

Fast Food

WHAT IS THE average amount of time spent on
preparing a meal at home?

A) 9 Minutes   **B)** 19 Minutes   **C)** 39 Minutes

Recipe for Disaster

WHAT ARE the odds that a cookbook is never
used to make a single one of its recommended
recipes?

A) 2/1   **B)** 4/1   **C)** 9/1

FOOD FOR THOUGHT & DRINK FOR PLEASURE

B) 11%

Although 100% of children know that cows produce milk, among Welsh youngsters aged 8 to 15, 11% did not know with which animal cheese is associated.

Source: Survey of 1,000+ children by Dairy Farmers of Britain (February 2007)

B) 19 Minutes

Ten years ago, over 25 minutes were spent preparing meals. We may have clipped 6 minutes off that, but that still seems like a very slow microwave to me. Anyway, toast is burned after 19 minutes, and beans take nowhere near that long to heat up.

Source: *Independent on Sunday* (12 February 2006)

A) 2/1

There are an estimated 171 million cookbooks on show in homes and kitchens throughout Britain. However, although an average family has access to 1,000 recipes, it will only ever try to make 35 of them, according to a survey for the UKTV Food Channel. The same survey revealed that a third of all cookbooks are displayed purely to make their owners 'look cool' and are never used for their designated purpose.

Source: *Daily Mail* (13 February 2006)

WHAT ARE THE ODDS?

Here's One I Didn't Prepare Earlier

WHAT PERCENTAGE of women are prepared to try a completely new recipe when making a meal?

A) 70% **B)** 33% **C)** 16%

Full of Beans

WHAT PERCENTAGE of Britons are regular coffee drinkers?

A) 28% **B)** 47% **C)** 64%

French Whine

WHAT PERCENTAGE of wine sold in Britain is French?

A) 19% **B)** 34% **C)** 51%

ANSWERS . . . .

A) **70%**

Women are reportedly almost three times as adventurous as men where food is concerned. Fewer than a third of men will experiment with a brand-new recipe, while 7 out of 10 women will give it a go.

Source: UKTV Food Channel (2006)

B) **47%**

Although that figure does include instant coffee, which as any coffee drinker will tell you is not the same thing at all. I think the question has to be asked: how do the other 53% ever wake up in the morning?

Source: *The Times* (8 March 2006)

A) **19%**

Just a decade ago the answer was 45%. And it's not just Britons who are turning their noses up at the French: in the USA the proportion of French wine drunk has slumped from 26% to 14% over the last ten years. But that hasn't stopped French vineyards demanding £2,000 a case for some of their top 2005 vintage clarets – a 100% mark-up on the previous year. *Sacre bleu!*

Source: *The Times* (10 February 2006)

Whose Round Is It?

WHAT PERCENTAGE of Britons are teetotal?

A) 1.5% **B)** 7% **C)** 13%

Fancy a Drink After Work?

WHAT PERCENTAGE of the average British pay packet went on alcohol in 2005?

A) 7% **B)** 14% **C)** 21%

Tipsy Truants

WHAT IS the chance that a school truant will claim the reason they are absent is because they have a hangover?

A) 1 in 16 **B)** 1 in 10 **C)** 1 in 3

B) 7%

Don't you just wince when someone tells you smugly that they are teetotal and will only have a 'fizzy water' and then won't buy a round because they're not drinking? Miserable saddo misers.

Source: *Observer* (December 2005)

A) 7%

In austere, post-war Britain 10% of the average pay packet was spent on alcohol in 1947, according to the Office for National Statistics. In our era of supposed 24-hour drinking and rampant booze-mania, it is down to 7%. The percentage spent on tobacco has dropped even further, from 12% to 3%.

Source: *Daily Mail* (14 December 2005)

A) 1 in 16

While 10% of children who played truant said they did so because they were bullied, 33% skipped lessons to go on a family holiday without their school's permission. But 6% admitted (boasted/claimed) that they had a hangover.

Source: *Daily Mail* (February 2006)

You Must Eat Your Greens . . . If We Give You Any

What percentage of child-minders supply a piece of fruit or some vegetables to their charges with the main meal or main snack every day?

A) 23%   **B)** 40%   **C)** 75%

___

Grubbing Around

WHAT PERCENTAGE of women in a US study admitted to keeping food in their office desks so that a snack would always be close at hand?

A) 25%   **B)** 50%   **C)** 75%

___

Tasty Choice

WHAT ARE the odds that a man would rather have food than sex?

A) 15/8   **B)** Evens   **C)** 10/1

FOOD FOR THOUGHT & DRINK FOR PLEASURE

ANSWERS . . . .

A) 23%

'What we were asking was pretty undemanding, which is why the results were so shocking,' said Pauline Nelson, co-author of a Leeds University report that quizzed both private and council-subsidised nurseries and child-minders. Nurseries, though, were twice as good as child-minders, with 46% of them handing out the healthy stuff (although there was no record of how much of it was actually eaten).

Source: *Daily Mail* (20 February 2006)

C) 75%

Women had four times more germs in, on and around their desks than men, found Professor Charles Gerba, and 75% of females admitted to treating their desks like larders.

Source: University of Arizona study (2007)

A) 15/8

Without, apparently, being given a choice of the food on offer, 34% (15/8) of the 800 men quizzed decided they'd rather be stuffing themselves than...

Source: Survey results by BMRB for Lighter Life (2007)

Is Tea Going to Pot?

**WHAT PROPORTION of cups of tea made in Britain
start life as a tea-bag rather than loose tea?**

A) 76%   **B)** 86%   **C)** 96%

TV Diners

**HOW MUCH more food is a toddler (ages 3 to 5)
likely to stuff down his or her throat while
watching a cartoon rather than eating with the
TV turned off?**

A) A Quarter   **B)** A Third   **C)** A Half

Booze Sorry Now?

**WHAT PERCENTAGE of Britain's drinkers would
find it 'difficult' to give up alcohol completely?**

A) 3%   **B)** 15%   **C)** 88%

FOOD FOR THOUGHT & DRINK FOR PLEASURE

C) 96%

Teapot sales have plummeted by 62% in the last five years, which is hardly surprising as only 4 cups in 100 are now made in the traditional way. Even more worrying is that sales of herbal teas have risen by 3.6% year on year. What is happening to dear old Britain? Next you'll be telling me that Lyons tea rooms have closed down.

Source: *Daily Telegraph* (3 April 2006)

B) A Third

A study appeared in the *Journal of the American Dietetic Association* which found that 'middle-class kids who habitually have meals at home while watching TV scoff a third more lunch when they are shown a cartoon while eating compared with when the goggle-box is turned off'. The explanation for this seemingly bizarre link went as follows: 'When children consistently view TV during meals it may distract them from normal fullness cues, which can lead to overeating.'

Source: *The Times* (8 April 2006)

C) 88%

Just 3% of 18–34-year-olds admit to drinking daily, whereas 15% of the over-55s (the largest proportion of any age group) said they liked a drink every day. However, 88% of all those questioned admitted they would have difficulty giving up the booze completely … even those abstemious 18-year-olds. Giving up is no problem for me – I do it regularly.

Source: *Guardian* (18 April 2006)

RISKY BUSINESS

'Women try their luck; men risk theirs.'
Oscar Wilde

Yo Ho Ho

A SHIP **carrying valuable cargo is most likely to be attacked by pirates in which of the following waters?**

A) Caribbean Sea   **B)** Aegean Sea   **C)** Indian Ocean

Driving to Kill

ASKED WHICH **they would brake or swerve to avoid, which of the following were drivers least likely to try to miss on the road?**

A) Rats   **B)** Pheasants   **C)** Cats

Going Down

HAD YOU **been one of the 851 male passengers on the *Titanic*, what were the odds that you survived post-iceberg?**

A) 5/1   **B)** 8/1   **C)** 12/1

ANSWERS . . . .

C) **Indian Ocean**

You probably haven't seen a ship flying the Jolly Roger other than in *Pirates of the Caribbean*, but modern-day buccaneers are out there – armed with guns, machetes, Uzis and dynamite. From the Caribbean and Aegean to the most dangerous waters around Indonesia (where 30 crew members were killed in 2004 alone), over 300 incidents of piracy are reported each year.

Source: Amnesty International 2005; *National Geographic* 2002

A) **Rats**

Only 32% of drivers would go out of their way to avoid hitting a rat; 47% would try to miss pheasants and 74% would endeavour not to deprive a cat of any its lives.

Source: Survey for Discovery Turbo TV Channel (March 2007)

A) **5/1**

The *Titanic* was much more of a disaster if you were unlucky enough to be male, as Leonardo DiCaprio could tell you. A staggering 709 men died, while just 142 survived (some of them later discovered in the lifeboats … dressed as women). How many people perished from boredom while watching the James Cameron movie has never been investigated.

Leap of Faith!

THERE ARE **about 350,000 skydivers in the US – an extreme sport that requires know-how, trust, and at least a bit of lunacy. What are the odds that a skydiver will fail to survive a leap?**

A) 6,700/1   **B)** 67,000/1   **C)** 670,000/1

Dead Man's Hand

WILD BILL HICKOK **was killed while holding pairs of black aces and black eights – hence the moniker 'Dead Man's Hand'. We assume your odds of being shot at the poker table are minimal, but what's the chance of being dealt this hand?**

A) 1 in 59   **B)** 1 in 5,900   **C)** 1 in 59,000

Mounting Challenges

IF YOU **were to grab a few bottles of oxygen and call for a Sherpa, what's the chance that you'd make it to the top of Mount Everest?**

A) Evens   **B)** Around 10/1   **C)** Around 20/1

RISKY BUSINESS

135

ANSWERS . . . .

B) 67,000/1

These folks have overcome their fear of flying, falling –
at about 120 mph – and dying! But with over two
million jumps a year, and an average of about 30
fatalities, there are fewer deaths from skydiving than
from scuba diving (90) or bee stings (46). Injuries can
be serious, but only about 1,200 were reported to the
US Parachute Association in 2002. And, about 4% of
jumpers are over 60!

Source: US Parachute Association (2002); *Skydiving* magazine; CDC

C) 1 in 59,000

Not a likely draw, unless you're spending a lot of time
at the poker table. Of course, Wild Bill probably would
have traded the hand for better odds on living. And
those might have improved significantly if he'd just
kept his back to the wall (as was his habit) and hadn't
already killed his murderer's brother.

Source: S. Verhoeven, *Britannica Almanac* (2005)

C) Around 20/1

First conquered in 1953, Everest has since attracted
several thousand brave or foolhardy souls desperate to
scale the almost 30,000-foot-high peak. Over 100 of
those have perished in the attempt and many remain
frozen on the mountain.

Source: *Everest News; National Geographic;* www.britannica.com

De-Constructed

WHEN YOU'RE putting up a building, which of the following workers is most likely to 'go down' on the job with a fatal injury?

A) A Carpenter   **B)** A Roofer   **C)** An Electrician

Wired?

THE FLYING WALLENDAS were renowned for their family high-wire act and especially their seven-person pyramid. When one man lost his footing 25 feet above the ground, causing them to fall, what were the chances that anyone survived?

A) 3 in 7   **B)** 5 in 7   **C)** 6 in 7

Tan Ban?

IT'S NO secret that overexposure to the sun can cause skin cancer. A 10% increase in exposure will increase your odds of developing a deadly melanoma by how much?

A) 5–9%   **B)** 12–15%   **C)** 16–19%

RISKY BUSINESS

137

A) A Carpenter

Carpenters, with a 37% rate of construction-site fatalities, are most likely to get nailed. Electricians are a very close second – just a wire away – at 36%. Roofers – with a good overview of everything – are at the low end with only 27% of fatal construction-site accidents.

Source: Bureau of Labor Statistics (2002)

B) 5 in 7

In 1962, unable to catch themselves, two fell to their deaths. The troupe returned to the scene of their catastrophe (Detroit) in 1998 for another attempt – which they performed safely 38 times over the following 17 days, proving once and for all that they were more balanced than most people had thought.

Source: www.wallenda.com (2005)

C) 16–19%

Skin cancer is the most common cancer in the US with an average of 1.3 million cases a year. Melanomas – just 4% of all skin cancers – cause 80% of all skin cancer deaths (7,400). Fair-skinned people are particularly susceptible, so limit your exposure to the sun – especially if you look like Michael Jackson.

Source: National Cancer Institute (2005)

WHAT ARE THE ODDS?

138

TRAVELLING THE LAND

'Once the travel bug bites, there is no known antidote, and I know that I shall be happily infected until the end of my life.'

Michael Palin

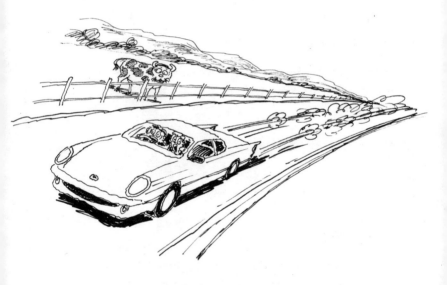

Destination Down Under?

WHAT PERCENTAGE of people emigrating from
Great Britain in 1913 ended up in Australia?

A) 42%   **B)** 17%   **C)** 5%

Where Am I?

HOW MUCH less likely than a woman is a man to
admit while driving that he is lost and to ask
for directions?

A) Half as Likely   **B)** As Likely   **C)** Twice as Likely

Scot Free

LANDING AT random on one of the hundreds of
islands dotted around Scotland, what are the
chances of finding that it is inhabited?

A) 5/1   **B)** 10/1   **C)** 20/1

TRAVELLING THE LAND

B) 17%

In 1913, the last year before the First World War, Great Britain alone parted with nearly 500,000 of its people. The Americas was the most popular destination, with 69% heading there. Australia came second, attracting 17%, and South Africa and 'other colonies' accounted for 5% each.

Source: *Cassells Book of Knowledge* (Waverley Book Company, 1923)

A) Half as Likely

Men drive women mad when they are at the wheel and find themselves in unfamiliar territory. On average it takes a woman ten minutes to realise, admit to and do something about the fact that she's lost. But, says a 2006 survey, it takes a man twice as long, twenty minutes, to pull over and seek help or even consult a map. The jury is still out as to whether Sat-Nav systems will eliminate such problems. Given that they have reportedly sent drivers the wrong way up one-way streets, down dead ends and into fords, we somehow doubt they will.

Source: RAC Direct Insurance (March 2006)

A) 5/1

Scotland has about 790 islands, but only about 130 are inhabited, so odds are you won't be invited in for a glass of whisky. Unless they boast very civilised sheep, that is.

Source: *UK 2005*

High But Not Dry

WHAT PERCENTAGE of Wales is above 305 metres?

A) 10%   **B)** 25%   **C)** 45%

Wandering Welsh

WHAT PERCENTAGE of people born in Wales are now living elsewhere?

A) 11%   **B)** 22%   **C)** 33%

Everybody Needs *Distant* Neighbours

POWYS IS the least densely populated region of Wales, with how many people per square kilometre?

A) 25   **B)** 125   **C)** 225

TRAVELLING THE LAND

143

B) 25%

'Wales is on the western side of Great Britain. It is mountainous – around one quarter is above 305 metres.' So why do they insist on making such a fuss about those valleys, one might reasonably ask?

Source: *UK 2005*

B) 22%

According to the most recent census (2001), of the 2.8 million UK residents who were born in Wales, almost a quarter are now living elsewhere. However, the population of Wales has remained virtually unchanged as a similar number of English and Scots have moved to Wales to take their place.

Source: *UK 2005*

A) 25

Driving through Powys to get to the annual Man versus Horse Marathon race held there in Llanwrtyd Wells, I swear I saw more sheep than people, but none of them was allowed to enter the race, which seemed a little unfair. Cardiff is the most densely populated part of Wales, with 2,269 people per square kilometre.

Source: *UK 2005*

Northern Light

WHAT PERCENTAGE of the population of the UK is Scottish?

A) 4.5%   **B)** 8.5%   **C)** 13%

Skye's the Limit

WHAT PERCENTAGE of Scots can speak Scottish Gaelic?

A) 1.2%   **B)** 12%   **C)** 30%

Wood You Believe It?

WHAT PERCENTAGE of Scotland's land area is covered by forest?

A) 6%   **B)** 16%   **C)** 26%

TRAVELLING THE LAND

B) 8.5%

Although Britain seems to have been run by Scots for the last decade (yes, even Tony Blair, despite those clipped tones, was born north of the border), less than a tenth of the UK population is Scottish.

Source: *UK 2005*

A) 1.2%

Introduced into Scotland in AD 500 and eventually becoming the dominant language, Scottish Gaelic now survives in just a few remote pockets, although in the Eielan Siar (formerly the Western Isles) Council Area, 60% of the population still speak it.

Source: *UK 2005*

B) 16%

Scotland accounts for 60% of Britain's conifer harvest and its sawmills churn out 42% of the UK's total lumber production.

Source: *UK 2005*

House That!

WHAT PROPORTION of dwellings in the UK are
semi-detached houses?

A) 22%   **B)** 27%   **C)** 31%

Ooh Arr

WHAT PERCENTAGE of the total UK land area is
agricultural land?

A) 55%   **B)** 66%   **C)** 77%

Well, Water You Know?

What percentage of the world's fresh surface
water is contained in Siberia's 400-mile-long,
5,315-foot-deep Lake Baikal?

A) 20%   **B)** 40%   **C)** 60%

TRAVELLING THE LAND

C) 31%

Suburbia rules – OK? Twenty-two per cent of dwellings are detached houses and 27% terraced. Without the UK's paranoia about semis and detached houses the world of situation comedy would have been very different and Hyacinth Bucket might never have become a household name.

Source: *UK 2005*

C) 77%

Bet that was a surprise, wasn't it, especially if, like most of us, you live in the middle of urban sprawl? In the UK most agricultural land is grassland or rough grazing, with just a quarter used to grow crops. Only around 40% of all the land in the EU is agricultural.

Source: *UK 2005*

A) 20%

The Earth's deepest lake holds more water than all of North America's Great Lakes combined ... but if a British water authority got control of it they could probably still manage to lose it all through leaks in a year or two!

Source: *Planet Earth* (BBC TV)

Motor Mouth

What percentage of British men admit to talking to their cars?

A) 12%   **B)** 25%   **C)** 37%

Service Breakdown

WHAT ARE the odds that a motorist will have to wait over an hour for his or her breakdown service to arrive?

A) 3/1   **B)** 6/1   **C)** 9/1

Brass-Neck Rubber-Neckers

WHAT PERCENTAGE of British motorists slow down to take a closer look at an accident they are driving past?

A) 33%   **B)** 66%   **C)** 99%

TRAVELLING THE LAND

149

ANSWERS . . . .

B) 25%

One in eight men give their cars names, while a quarter enjoy the odd conversation with their metal partners. What do they say, then? 'How are you feeling?' 'Where have you been on holiday?' 'Isn't the price of petrol shameful?' Or, perhaps, 'How stupid am I for talking to an inanimate mechanised object?'

Source: eBay Motors (2006)

A) 3/1

'Almost one in four drivers has to wait more than an hour before help arrives,' according to a Which? report. Well, that's not bad, in my opinion, given that it often takes longer than that to get through to a human being in any large company's call centre.

Source: *Daily Mail* (6 April 2006)

B) 66%

A quarter of people involved in crashes said that they 'felt embarrassed' by the staring of fellow motorists. You might have thought they'd have more important things to worry about. The Scots are the UK's champion rubber-neckers (or maybe just the most honest), with 78% of them admitting to it, while Londoners were the least likely to gawp (presumably because crashes are hardly a rare occurrence in the capital). But overall 'two in three motorists' admitted rubbernecking, while an astonishing 10% admitted to stopping to get a better view – and 1 in 20 had caused another crash because of their staring!

Source: Press Association (April 2006)

WHAT ARE THE ODDS?

150

Who Could Afford to Live There?

THE BIGGEST property price rise in Britain in the last decade was 268%. But where did it take place?

A) Ceredigion   **B)** Cornwall   **C)** Isle of Anglesey

Don't Be a Clot

BY WHAT percentage will wearing tight, knee-length socks on a long-haul flight reduce the chance of suffering from deep vein thrombosis?

A) 30%   **B)** 60%   **C)** 90%

On the Way to Nowhere

WHAT ARE the odds that a driver has been sent on a wild goose chase by his or her car satellite navigation system?

A) 6/4   **B)** 4/1   **C)** 9/1

TRAVELLING THE LAND

ANSWERS . . . .

B) Cornwall

Ceredigion clocked in third with its average price up from £48,137 to £165,663. In second place was Anglesey, where you will now have to pay an average of £158,527, rather than 1996's £44,998. But the biggest ten-year rise was in Cornwall, where average prices have rocketed from £53,081 to £195,308. None of these places comes close to being the most expensive region in Britain, though. That dubious honour is still held by Surrey – with an average property now costing £298,835, as opposed to £98,566 in 1996.

Source: Halifax (April 2006)

C) 90%

With up to 100,000 suffering from DVT, 8,000 of them after long-haul flights, and up to 100 people a year dying from it, a study of 2,637 such passengers showed that 47 not wearing the socks contracted the condition but only 3 of the sock-wearers did likewise.

Source: Study by Cochrane Library, Oxford Medical Research Body (April 2006)

A) 6/4

38% of drivers surveyed said they had used a sat-nav system, of which 25% said that after having problems they used the system less or not at all, with 40% (6/4) claiming to have got lost or delayed whilst using sat-nav.

Source: Survey by www.which.co.uk (2007)

First-Class Fib

WHAT PERCENTAGE of people would lie about precisely where they live in order to make themselves appear more upmarket?

A) 40%   **B)** 60%   **C)** 80%

Screwed Up

WHAT ARE the odds that when you move into your new dream home, the previous residents will have unscrewed and removed the light fittings?

A) 3/1   **B)** 5/1   **C)** 8/1

Green with Envy?

QUESTIONED ABOUT their contribution towards protecting the environment, what were the odds that someone said they had deliberately decided against a holiday which involved flying?

A) 3/1   **B)** 8/1   **C)** 11/1

TRAVELLING THE LAND

153

A) **40%**

In a survey of 2,000 home-owners, some 80% said that they would trade in their current home for a not so good one in a better neighbourhood, while 2 in 5 were prepared to say that they lived in a different area from the one they actually occupied, for snobbish reasons.

Source: Ipsos MORI (May 2006)

C) **8/1**

Five per cent of householders take their wheelie bins with them when they depart a house they have sold; 25% take plants from the garden. But 12% are so retentive – or tight – that they unscrew the light fittings.

Source: Halifax (May 2006)

A) **3/1**

Although we are prepared to suffer a little dimness in the evening, with 75% of us now using low-energy light bulbs, most of us aren't prepared to forgo our weeks in the sun, as only 24% of those surveyed said that they had given up their holiday air travel.

Source: *Guardian* (February 2006)

CRIME & PUNISHMENT

'You can get much farther with a kind word and a gun than you can with a kind word alone.'

Al Capone

Rock Stars

ALCATRAZ, **the maximum-security prison in San Francisco Bay, once housed the US's most violent criminals. Of the 36 inmates who attempted to break out of 'The Rock', what were their odds of succeeding?**

A) 6/1   **B)** 3/1   **C)** Zero

Minimum Security?

US PRISONS **house about 25% of the world's total prison population. Chances are that you'll find about 11% of these inmates confined in which level of prison security?**

A) Low/Minimum   **B)** Medium   **C)** High/Maximum

Wheel Risk?

YOUR CAR **is likely to be stolen once every ...**

A) 7 Years   **B)** 47 Years   **C)** 77 Years

CRIME & PUNISHMENT

ANSWERS . . . .

C) **Zero**

Home to such notables as Al Capone, 'Birdman' Robert Stroud and Machine-Gun Kelly, Alcatraz, in its 29 years as the US's premier 'No Exit' federal pen, had 14 escape attempts involving 36 inmates: 22 were caught and returned; 7 were shot and killed; and 2 drowned. The five listed as 'never found' were presumed to have perished in the cold, turbulent, shark-infested waters surrounding The Rock.

Source: National Park Service 2005

C) **High/Maximum**

The razor wire and cement toilets of maximum security are for the worst of the worst 11%. Another 25% are housed in medium-security digs. The really well-behaved and white-collar perps (around 60%) can stroll through minimum-security grounds, do some network-ing – with the chance of meeting politicians, occa-sional celebs, or domestic divas – and start planning partnerships for their futures on the outside.

Source: Bureau of Prisons 2005

C) **77 Years**

Cars aged between 11 and 15 years old are more likely to be stolen than those 3 years old or less, with 13-year-old cars statistically being most at risk – with a 30/1 chance of being nicked. So don't be worried if you've got a nice, shiny Merc parked outside; the car thieves are much more likely to target your neighbour's rust bucket down the road. But either way, on average you'll be too old to drive anyway by the time you have a car stolen for the first time.

Source: *UK 2005*

Judge Me By My Ability

WHAT ARE the odds of a British judge having attended a private school?

A) 55%   B) 68%   C) 76%

Open Door Policy?

AND IN which UK city are you most likely to be burgled?

A) Leeds   B) Hull   C) Nottingham

Now Do You Promise Not to Do It Again?

WHAT PERCENTAGE of burglars who are apprehended are cautioned rather than being taken to court?

A) 3%   B) 13%   C) 29.6%

159

ANSWERS . . . .

C) 76%

Only 7% of all children attend private schools, but research by the Sutton Trust education charity, unveiled in June 2006, showed that 55% of solicitors; 68% of barristers and 76% of judges had done so.

Source: *Daily Mail* (15 June 2006)

C) Nottingham

Londoners are 29.1% more likely than average to claim on their insurance for household theft, but Leeds comes in as the third worst at 65.8% more likely. Hull is the runner-up with 88.5% more claims than average. But Nottingham has the dubious honour of topping the list with 109.4% more claims than the UK average.

Source: Endsleigh Insurance (April 2006)

B) 13%

Householders everywhere will be less than delighted to learn that while 756,000 burglaries were committed in 2004–5, just 15,283 house-breakers were caught, and then 2,044 of them were let off with a caution. The statistics also showed that of 172,551 people convicted of theft and handling stolen goods, 61,944, or 36%, were merely cautioned. So much for the old adage that the only problem with a life of crime is getting caught. That's not even a problem these days.

Source: *Daily Mail* (15 April 2006)

WHAT ARE THE ODDS?

POLITICS & WORLD EVENTS

'In politics, if you want anything said, ask a man. If you want anything done, ask a woman.'

Margaret Thatcher

Napoleonic Plague

ON THE five-month march to invade Russia in 1812, what were the chances of Napoleon's troops dying from disease, even before the battles began?

A) 10%   **B)** 20%   **C)** 40%

Crap Question

HOW MANY times was the word 'crap' uttered in Parliament from the start of 2002 until June 2006?

A) 1   **B)** 13   **C)** 23

Free to Be

WHAT ARE the chances that anyone living on Earth today lives in a democratic nation?

A) 17 in 100   **B)** 37 in 100   **C)** 57 in 100

C) 40%

Through dysentery, diarrhoea and an array of other ailments, over a third of Napoleon's 500,000 troops ended up with lives as short as their leader. And that was before the fighting started! When they finally reached Moscow, the Russians had already razed it to the ground, so there was nothing left to conquer. By the end of the campaign (the retreat was even worse than the advance for the soldiers), only 20,000 of the original half a million troops survived.

Source: G. C. Kohn, ed., *Encyclopedia of Plague & Pestilence, Facts on File* (1995)

B) 13

The word had to be considered for inclusion on the list of words banned by The Speaker after Lib Dem MP Roger Williams was scolded for using it in June 2006, apparently the 13th occasion it had been spoken in that place since 2002.

Source: 'People' column, *The Times* (15 June 2006)

C) 57 in 100

Buoyed by India's huge electorate of over a billion, the majority of people worldwide can now claim to live in some form of democratic society. But before we break out into paroxysms of democratic self-congratulation, let's remember that there are still some 3 billion people in the world who are disenfranchised, save for their local version of *X Factor* or *Big Brother*.

Source: UN Human Development Report

Rude Britania

MUMBAI IN India was voted the rudest city in the world, registering just 32% for politeness, while New York came top with 80%. What did London score?

A) 67% **B)** 57% **C)** 37%

Collateral Damage

WHAT WERE the odds that a death attributable to the Second World War's European and Pacific campaigns was that of a civilian?

A) 2/1 **B)** Evens **C)** 1/2

White Anglo-Saxon Presidents

SO FAR, the spectrum of US presidents has ranged from white to white, male to male, and one form of Christianity to another. But which of the following denominations has been most likely to provide a US president?

A) Methodist **B)** Presbyterian **C)** Episcopalian

B) 57%

2,000 courtesy tests were carried out in 35 different cities, revealing that London came joint fifteenth in the poll, alongside its near neighbour Paris, and that people in both countries were equally obnoxious, notching up a score of 57% – 10% behind Auckland and Warsaw; but 20% ahead of Kuala Lumpur. Rudest city ever encountered was Moscow twenty years ago, where waiters refused admission to empty restaurants. Nothing much seems to have changed. It managed just 42%.

Source: Reader's Digest Survey (June 2006)

C) 1/2

Just over two-thirds of all deaths in the Second World War were of civilians. No wonder so many of our enemies (there were a good dozen of them, by the way, not just Germany, Italy and Japan) joined the military – maybe it was the safest place to be.

Source: www.world-war-2.info

C) Episcopalian

The Episcopal Church has been the Church of choice for 11 presidents. Six Presbyterians have become top dog, as have five Methodists. With the election of JFK, the Catholic barrier was finally broken after nearly 200 years.

Source: www.whitehouse.gov

WHAT ARE THE ODDS?

Unreconstructed

WHAT ARE the chances that an average Alabama resident voted to retain the state's constitutional ban on interracial marriage in the year 2000?

A) 25%   **B)** 40%   **C)** 65%

See You, Gordon

WHAT PERCENTAGE of people in the UK believe that it is wrong for a Scot to be Prime Minister as Scotland has its own parliament?

A) 52%   **B)** 55%   **C)** 67%

New Day Off

WHAT PERCENTAGE of people polled thought that D Day would be the best occasion for a new national holiday?

A) 14%   **B)** 21%   **C)** 27%

POLITICS & WORLD EVENTS

ANSWERS . . . .

B) 40%

Sweet home, Alabama? Even though the bill lifting the
ban on miscegenation did pass, 2 in every 5
Alabamians still voted to preserve it – a full 33 years
after the US Supreme Court ruled it unconstitutional!

Source: Alabama Education Association (2003)

A) 52%

While 55% of English people believe it is wrong for a
Scot to be Prime Minister, 52% of people in the whole
of the UK gave that answer.

Source: ICM poll – *Daily Telegraph* (20 June 2006)

A) 14%

Top of the days which deserve to be celebrated via a
national holiday was the signing of the Magna Carta
(15 June 1215) which picked up 27% of the vote,
ahead of the 21% won by supporters of VE Day (8 May
1945), leaving D Day (6 June 1944) trailing in third
with 14%. Sadly, the anniversary of Luton Town's
League Cup triumph failed to register.

Source: *BBC History* magazine survey (May 2006)

Out of This World

IN 1962, what odds were given by a bookie on a human being walking on the surface of the moon before 1 January 1970?

A) 10/1   **B)** 100/1   **C)** 1,000/1

Sexy Politics

WHERE DID Tory leader David Cameron finish in a 2006 poll of 'Top 100 Sexiest People in the World'?

A) 92nd   **B)** 69th   **C)** 47th

Survival of the Witless?

WHAT ARE the chances that a US state currently has a law challenging the validity of evolution 'theory'?

A) 3 in 50   **B)** 11 in 50   **C)** 17 in 50

POLITICS & WORLD EVENTS

C) 1,000/1

David Threlfall called into the headquarters of William Hill in 1962 to ask what odds they would give him and probably couldn't believe his luck when he was told 1,000/1. Clearly he knew more than the bookie about the final frontier and invested a tenner (more than a week's wages) there and then. Seven years later, in July 1969 when Neil Armstrong made his 'one small step', Threlfall duly collected ten grand. A happy ending? Not quite. He splashed out on a sports car with his winnings, and later died in a road accident while driving the vehicle.

Source: William Hill

A) 92nd

OK, he may not quite be in Brad Pitt's league, but can you imagine his two predecessors – Iain Duncan Smith and Michael Howard – getting into the top 1000? And Cameron even finished ahead of singer James Blunt and Russell Crowe! Clearly the readers of *New Woman* really are new women.

Source: *New Woman* (February 2006)

C) 17 in 50

Let Darwin, Darrow, and Galileo burn in hell! So sayeth voters in 17 states out to thwart the teaching of the science of evolution with a variety of tactics, including warning labels in high school biology books. Strangely, no compromise is in the works to label both evolution *and* the Bible as 'theories' or agree on the possibility that God rested on the seventh day to let things *evolve*.

Source: www.tolerance.org

Reign Fall?

WHAT PERCENTAGE of *New Statesman* readers asked whether Britain will ever become a republic? answered 'Yes'?

A) 28%   **B)** 56%   **C)** 72%

Tongue Tied

WHAT PERCENTAGE of the world's 6,750 known languages are actively spoken by fewer than 100,000 people?

A) 30%   **B)** 60%   **C)** 90%

A Show of Hands

IN WHICH of the following countries are you most likely to have to bribe a government official to get something done?

A) Colombia   **B)** Turkey   **C)** Finland

POLITICS & WORLD EVENTS

171

C) 72%

But if we do become a republic, who will be president? No doubt Robbie Williams, Elton John, Lewis Hamilton, David Beckham, Davina McCall and Wayne Rooney would be among the front-runners. Still think all those *New Statesman* readers have the right idea?

Source: *New Statesman* (1 May 2006)

C) 90%

It used to be a lot more than 6,750, though. One language becomes officially extinct every fortnight, and 350 have 50 or fewer speakers, so won't be around for much longer. The most prolific language is Mandarin, with 1 billion speakers. English comes second, spoken by 508 million. Double Dutch is still widespread.

Source: *The Indypedia* (2006)

B) Turkey

Turkey ranks 77th on the world's corruption index, below the drug-fuelled economy of Colombia (59th) and well back of the not-so-perfect US (18th) – but all three are well ahead of Haiti and Bangladesh, tied for last place at 145th. But you'll never have to slip a Finn a fin: Finland is the Earth's least corrupt nation. Or maybe that's just what they've conned us into thinking – after all, Finns ain't what they used to be!

Source: Transparency International Corruption Perceptions Index 2004

ANSWERS ➤

Good TV? That's Debatable

WHAT ARE the chances that a TV viewer has ever watched the BBC Parliament channel?

A) 100/1   **B)** 1,000/1   **C)** 10,000/1

Lost Deposits

WHAT PERCENTAGE of the votes cast must a candidate at a General Election poll in order to avoid losing his or her deposit?

A) 1%   **B)** 5%   **C)** 10%

That's a Worry

WHAT PERCENTAGE of British males claim they are kept awake at night worrying about what George Bush is up to?

A) 1.9%   **B)** 5.6%   **C)** 9.2%

C) 10,000/1

And the channel can hardly take comfort from the few who *do* bother to tune in. Of those who watch, just 1 in 500 turns on for 15 minutes or more each week – so that'll be Messrs Blair, Brown, Cameron, Campbell, then …

Source: BARB (March 2006)

B) 5%

The late Screaming Lord Sutch, for many years the leader of the Official Monster Raving Loony Party, stood for Parliament on a record 41 occasions. He lost his deposit on a record 41 occasions. That wasn't cheap fun, as the deposit currently stands at £500.

Source: Graham Sharpe, *The Man Who Was Screaming Lord Sutch* (Aurum Press, 2005)

B) 5.6%

Yes, we thought it would be more, too! Are there any bigger worries in the world than what Dubbya is planning? You would think at least half the country would be kept awake just trying to work out what he means in speeches such as this one: 'We look forward to analysing and working with legislation that will make – it would hope – put a free press's mind at ease that you're not being denied information you shouldn't see.'

Source: Survey by pillow manufacturer John Cotton (2005)

ON THE
RECORD

'Music is the art which is most nigh to tears and memory.'

Oscar Wilde

Stoned

WHAT WERE the odds that a Rolling Stones single would top the charts between 1963 and 1971?

A) 3/1   **B)** 2/1   **C)** Evens

Yeah, Yeah, Yeah

WHAT PERCENTAGE of the Beatles' *Billboard* US Top 40 hits prior to 2007 reached number one?

A) 24%   **B)** 38%   **C)** 74%

The Brits

WHAT PROPORTION of albums bought in Britain in 2005 were the work of British artists?

A) About 50%   **B)** About 25%   **C)** About 10%

ON THE RECORD

ANSWERS . . . .

C) Evens

The Rolling Stones enjoyed 16 Top 30 single hits
between July 1963 (when 'Come On' charted) and
April 1971 (when 'Brown Sugar' was a smash). Of the
16, 'It's All Over Now' (in July 1964) was the first and
'Honky Tonk Women' (in July 1969) the last of their
eight number ones.

Source: *Guinness World Record British Hit Singles & Albums*

B) 38%

Only 20 of the Beatles' 52 Top 40 hits made it to the
top, partly because the former Quarrymen became victims of their own success. Some Beatles hits stalled at
number 2 or 3 because their path to the top was
blocked by other Beatles songs. In fact, during one
week in 1964, the Beatles simultaneously held the top
5 spots on the chart! No, 'mania' was not too strong a
word.

Source: *The* Billboard *Book of Top 40 Hits*, 7th edn

A) About 50%

In fact 49.4% of all albums sold in the UK in 2005
were made by UK artists, and all five of the bestselling
albums of the year were by home grown, er, talent:
James Blunt's *Back to Bedlam*; Coldplay's *X&Y*; Robbie
Williams's *Intensive Care*; Kaiser Chiefs' *Employment*;
and Gorillaz's *Demon Days*

Source: *Guardian* (13 February 2006)

How Much?!

WHAT WAS the cost (face value) of the most expensive concert ticket sold in the world in 2005?

A) £245   **B)** £390   **C)** £495

Monkeying Around

WHAT PERCENTAGE of all albums sold in Britain between 21 and 28 January 2006 were by the Arctic Monkeys.

A) 5.2%   **B)** 12.5%   **C)** 16.4%

Queen Larry

HOW MUCH would you have to pay for a copy of Freddie Mercury's obscure 1973 single 'I Can Hear Music'?

A) £50   **B)** £200   **C)** £600

ON THE RECORD

179

ANSWERS . . . .

A) £245

U2 at Twickenham? The Rolling Stones in Madison Square Garden? Oh no. You had to shell out 245 quid to see the Eagles in Melbourne, which makes you wonder when anyone last bothered touring Down Under. Top whack tickets for the Stones in London by August 2007 were £495, while French fans shelled out up to £390 to see Barbra Streisand in June of that year.

Source: *Guardian* (13 February 2006)

C) 16.4%

In the week of their debut album's release, the new darlings of the British music scene managed to break the record for the fastest-selling album of all time in this country. Not bad for four Northern lads with dodgy haircuts.

B) £200

The odds are you won't be able to find one, but if you can, it will set you back at least 200 quid (or more if you get carried away bidding for a copy on eBay). It was released on the EMI label under the delightful pseudonym Larry Lurex. Before handing over the cash, be sure that the centre of the 7-inch is not solid, rather than press-out, then you'll know you've got a genuine version rather than a counterfeit.

Source: *Rare Record Price Guide* (2008)

Yanks a Lot

WHO MAKES the most money annually by allowing their music to be used in advertisements in the US?

A) The Kinks   **B)** The Rolling Stones   **C)** The Who

That's a Classic

WHAT PERCENTAGE of an album has to be classified as 'classical' in order for the record to be eligible for inclusion in the Classical Albums Chart?

A) 100%   **B)** 80%   **C)** 60%

Cold Reception

WHEN THE Monster Raving Loony Party ran a poll in March 2006 asking what people would like to see banned what percentage of respondents voted for 'Bands like Coldplay'?

A) 23.5%   **B)** 15.0%   **C)** 3.8%

ON THE RECORD

181

A) **The Kinks**

The Who have made £2 million by providing the soundtrack for Nissan and 7-Up, among others. The cash-strapped Stones generated £2.3 million, primarily through their agreement with Microsoft. Way out in front, though, are Ray Davies and co., who clock up £6 million each year but have to hear their music advertising everything from IBM computers to Tide washing powder.

Source: *Sunday Times* (12 March 2006)

C) **60%**

Popular tenor Vittorio Grigolo's 2006 album *In the Hands of Love* leapt into the UK Album Chart at number 6, so you would have expected it to soar straight to the top of the Classical Album Chart. However, the Classical Advisory Panel (yes, there really is such an organisation) ruled that only 5 of its 14 tracks were classical, leaving it 22.5% light of the requirement set by the Official Charts Company. I bought the album for a tenner! Sorry.

A) **23.5%**

Some may say that those 23.5% should have their party membership revoked, as clearly they are not in the least 'loony'. 'Superglue' was unpopular with 3.8%, while 15% opted for 'Politicians'.

Source: Monster Raving Loony Party (March 2006)

ART &
POP
CULTURE

'Culture is roughly anything we do and the monkeys don't.'

Lord Raglan

Hot Properties

WHICH OF these blockbuster toy phenomena has defied the odds and sold continuously for over twenty years?

A) Care Bears **B)** Cabbage Patch Kids **C)** Furbies

Radio Raves

EVEN FOR those of you plugged into iPods, radio is still a must-have medium. If you stopped a car at random on almost any street in the US, the odds are that the radio would be tuned to which of the following?

A) Country Music **B)** Oldies **C)** News/Talk

Cartoon Culture

WHAT ARE the odds that a British parent voted for *The Simpsons* as the top cartoon of all time?

A) 8% **B)** 12% **C)** 23%

ANSWERS . . . .

B) Cabbage Patch Kids

Despite predictions that the appeal of these homely kids would fade after the first riotous year in 1983, they've gone on to sell over $5 *billion* in dolls and associated merchandise. Care Bears, another 1980s phenomenon, were successfully revived in 2002, after a long absence. As for Furbies, they're still in the pantheon of hot toys, jabbering in Furbish among themselves.

Source: Schlaifer Nance & Co (2005)

A) Country Music

It's not just hillbillies' 'country' any more – even though thinking of George Clooney in *Oh, Brother, Where Art Thou?* is enough to bring on a lot of gap-toothed smiles. With over 2000 stations nationwide, country music is still ahead of news/talk's often blood-boiling 1300 stations and the 800 or so broadcasting oldies.

Source: *World Almanac* (2005)

C) 23%

Homer, Bart, Marge et al romped home top of the cartoon pops with 23% of the vote, beating runners-up *Shrek* with 15% and *Tom and Jerry* with 12%.

Source: CBBC (July 2006)

WHAT ARE THE ODDS?

Dead Endings

IF YOU were a victim in one of Agatha Christie's Miss Marple mysteries, you were most likely to have been done in by which of the following?

A) Poisoning   **B)** Strangling   **C)** Gunshot

Alas, Poor Yorick

WHEN WILL SHAKESPEARE sat down to write, what were the odds he'd be working on a comedy?

A) About 1/2   **B)** Almost Evens   **C)** Almost 2/1

In Like Clint

WHAT ARE the chances that a 1970s Clint Eastwood movie features the actor as a cop or a cowboy?

A) 4 in 15   **B)** 8 in 15   **C)** 12 in 15

ART & POP CULTURE

187

A) Poisoning

Of the 26 murders Miss Marple solved in her 12 out-ings in print, there were 9 poisonings, 7 stranglings, 5 gunshot wounds, 1 crushing by rocks (ouch!) and 4 bludgeonings. If you're travelling in the English countryside, you might want to leave St Mary Mead off your itinerary.

Source: www.agathachristie.com (2005)

B) Almost Evens

Of the 38 plays attributed to Shakespeare, 18 are comedies – allegedly. If you don't recall anything funny from your English class, maybe you were studying one of the 10 tragedies, or the 10 histories. Or maybe you didn't understand a word of what you were reading. To be or not to be? No, I don't get it. Where's the punchline?

Source: Folger Library; www.shakespeare.com (2005)

B) 8 in 15

With three turns as Dirty Harry, as well as several other cop and cowpoke roles, Clint spent most of the 1970s looking tough and clutching a weighty firearm. But Eastwood also showed his softer side in films like *Play Misty for Me* and *The Bridges of Madison County*, in addi-tion to *Million Dollar Baby*, which earned him Oscars for Best Director and Best Picture in 2004.

Source: www.imdb.com

Which Way Out

OF THE FOLLOWING, **which is the most likely cause of the premature death of a major rock and roller?**

A) Plane Crash   **B)** Traffic Accident   **C)** Bizarre Accident

---

Laughing Matters

FROM **W.C. Fields to Jim Carrey and Jack Nicholson, Hollywood has turned out a lot of jokers. But what's the chance of a comedy being awarded the Oscar for Best Picture?**

A) 1 in 5   **B)** 1 in 10   **C)** 1 in 20

Bald Ambition

WHAT'S THE **likelihood of director Alfred Hitchcock appearing in one of his own films?**

A) 61%   **B)** 89%   **C)** 100%

C) Bizarre Accident

Bizarre accidents seem to be the rule among rockers –
and not just for Spinal Tap drummers. Among the freak,
career-ending occurrences are Chet Baker's defenestration
(being thrown out of a window), Mama Cass's choking
on a ham sandwich (widely reported but not confirmed)
and Beach Boy Dennis Wilson's accidental drowning. Let's
not dwell on Elvis and his junk-food-fuelled demise.

Source: *Fuller Up; The Dead Musicians' Directory; Schott's Original Miscellany*
(2004)

B) 1 in 10

At the time of writing, only seven comedies have ever
won Best Picture. *Seven!* Can the Academy really take
themselves that seriously? The most recent was *Annie
Hall* in 1977. The others: *It Happened One Night* (1934),
You Can't Take It With You (1938), *Going My Way*
(1944), *The Apartment* (1960), *Tom Jones* (1963) and (at
a push) *The Sting* (1973). No Marx Brothers! No *Some
Like It Hot* or *M*A*S*H* or *As Good As It Gets*. It's no
wonder Woody Allen's neurotic.

Source: Alexander and Associates/Video Flash

C) 100%

That's right, the Master of Suspense was also the Master
of I'm-Going-to-Be-in-Every-One-of-My-41-Pictures. He
usually made his appearance just when you'd stopped
looking for him. But how, you may wonder, did he
find his way into *Lifeboat*, a movie which featured just
10 actors and no extras? Hitchcock's before and after
photos were on the back of a prop newspaper, in an ad
for 'Reduco Obesity Slayer'.

Source: http://hitchcock.tv/cam/cameos.html

Just William

WHAT ARE the odds that a word used by Shakespeare will appear only once in his writings?

A) 3.8/1 **B)** 38/1 **C)** 380/1

Wise Move?

WHAT ARE the odds that book-buying Londoners will purchase at least one volume 'solely in order to look intelligent'?

A) 2/1 **B)** 8/1 **C)** 25/1

Wrong Number

WHAT ARE the odds that a London theatre-goer has been disturbed by someone's mobile phone ringing during a performance?

A) 5/4 **B)** 9/4 **C)** 11/4

ART & POP CULTURE

191

A) 3.8/1

'It has been calculated that Shakespeare, who had a very wide vocabulary, used not more than 24,000 words in his writings, and 5,000 of those he used only once.' Who said Shakespeare scholars have too much time on their hands?

Source: *Cassells Book of Knowledge* (1923)

A) 2/1

Which means that 66% claim they have never bought a book just to look smart. Who are they trying to kid? They all finished *A Brief History of Time*, then, did they? And *Zen and the Art of Motorcycle Maintenance*? And *The Da Vinci Code*? Oh, wait a minute, there were plenty of other reasons for not finishing that one.

Source: *The Indypedia* (2006)

A) 5/4

Actor Richard Griffiths stopped performances of *The History Boys* in both London and New York when mobiles went off, earning standing ovations in the process. 44% of London theatre-goers have suffered, and 72% want technology to block calls in theatres.

Source: Survey by *The Stage* newspaper (September 2006)

Take It as Read

WHAT PERCENTAGE of authors in the Top 20 most
frequently borrowed from public libraries
between 1996 and 2006 were female?

A) 57%   **B)** 50%   **C)** 33%

Pirates of the Caribbean?

WHAT ARE the odds that the DVD you buy is a
bootleg?

A) 2/1   **B)** 10/1   **C)** 33/1

Tout of Order

WHAT PERCENTAGE of tickets for concerts in the
UK end up on the black market?

A) 15%   **B)** 20%   **C)** 35%

ART & POP CULTURE

193

ANSWERS . . . .

A) 57%

There are actually 21 authors in the Top 20, as co-authors of children's books Janet and Allan Ahlberg figure at number 6 on the list. Of the remaining 19, topped by Catherine Cookson and tailed by Lucy Daniels, 11 are female. Top male author, at number 3, was American comic horror writer, R. L. Stine. Jeffrey Archer failed to make the list, but probably had more important things to worry about in those years anyway.

Source: Public Lending Right (March 2006)

A) 2/1

One DVD sale in three is now a bootleg copy – making the British market the second worst in the world for piracy. Only the USA has a higher rate of illicit copying.

Source: *The Times* (23 March 2006)

B) 20%

Reporter David Rose said, 'a fifth of all concert tickets in the UK are estimated to be resold after their initial purchase'. At least black market touts rip you off honestly, though, quoting an all-in price rather than adding booking fees and service charges, and making you book through premium-rated phone lines!

Source: *The Times* (28 April 2006)

SPORTS:
FEATS &
DEFEATS

'Life isn't about winning, it's about having the grace to learn about yourself, and by pitting yourself against the challenges of sport you learn about what sort of person you are.'

Lynn Davies

Dover Souls

IT MAY be our favourite overseas holiday destination, but there are easier ways to get there! What is the chance of success when attempting the 21-mile Channel swim from England to France?

A) 1 in 5   **B)** 2 in 5   **C)** 3 in 5

_____

The Vision Thing

BASED ON participant percentages, in which of the following sports are you most likely to suffer an eye injury?

A) Badminton   **B)** Baseball   **C)** Boxing

_____

Do Sporty Girls Team Up?

WHAT ARE the odds that a woman in the UK takes part in team or competitive sport?

A) 75/1   **B)** 55/1   **C)** 35/1

SPORTS: FEATS & DEFEATS

197

ANSWERS . . . .

B) 2 in 5

About 40% of those attempting to swim the 15°C
Channel from Dover to Calais actually go all the way.
At the time of writing, the record for the swim is
Christof Wandratsch's 7 hours 3 minutes, set in 2005.
Roughly twice as many men as women have made the
crossing, although Alison Streeter MBE (presumably for
services to the goose-fat industry) leaves everyone else
standing when it comes to successful attempts, with an
amazing 43. She once went there, and back, and there
again, without taking a break! David Walliams did it
for charity in 2006.

Source: Channel Swimming Association

A) Badminton

Everyone's favourite back-garden pastime is actually
the most dangerous sport in terms of eye injuries.
Maybe no one's paying attention because they're all
too busy giggling at the word 'shuttlecock'.

Source: CDC; NCHS 2004

C) 35/1

3.8 million women take part in regular sport in the UK,
compared with 4.7 million men, and it is a 35/1 shot
that any woman is engaged in team or competitive
sport. 19% of UK women name walking as their main
sporting activity.

Source: *Observer Sports Monthly* (May 2007)

Call the Fall

THERE'S NEVER been a fighter to equal
Muhammad Ali – not least in his ability to call
the round of an opponent's fall. In which round
of a fight was Ali most likely to deliver a KO?

A) Round 5   **B)** Round 7   **C)** Round 12

For Love or Money?

OF THE following tennis greats, which one had
the best odds of winning Wimbledon during the
best ten years of his career?

A) John McEnroe   **B)** Björn Borg   **C)** Pete Sampras

Botham's Batterings

IN A TOTAL of 161 Test innings, what were the
odds that Ian Botham would not be got out by
the opposition?

A) 11/1   **B)** 26/1   **C)** 39/1

B) Round 7

In 61 fights, Ali won by knockout on 37 occasions, 7 of them occurring in the 7th round. He got 5 in the 3rd and 3 in the 12th. Oddly enough, he never won by knockout in the 6th, 9th, 10th or 13th rounds.

Source: www.ali.com

C) Pete Sampras

Borg was close behind with five wins in a row between 1976 and 1980, but Sampras was practically unstoppable, winning 7 of 10 championship matches between 1993 and 2002. McEnroe, entertaining on and off the court, screamed his way to just three victories in 1981, 1983 and 1984, but unlike Sampras and Borg, he played in (and won) the doubles tournament, too.

Source: www.wimbledon.com (2005)

B) 26/1

Sir Ian Botham was the Freddie Flintoff of his day, a swashbuckling all-rounder who always had the cricket crowd holding its breath when he came out to bat. He liked to entertain by hitting sixes and fours, and he took a lot more chances than most batsmen, so it's hardly surprising that throughout his international career, and in spite of coming in well down the order, he was not out only six times.

Source: Christopher Martin-Jones, *World Crickets* (OUP, 1996)

The Power behind the Thrown

WHICH OF the following objects is most likely to have been thrown more than 80 metres in a men's Olympic competition?

A) A Discuss   **B)** A Hammer   **C)** A Dwarf

Read All About It – Or Not

WHAT ARE the odds that an article in the sports pages of your national newspaper will be about a women's event?

A) 91/1   **B)** 19/1   **C)** 19/2

Strike While the Whistle is Shrill

WHAT ARE the odds of the first goal in a football match being scored within 10 minutes of kick-off?

A) 12/1   **B)** 8/1   **C)** 4/1

SPORTS: FEATS & DEFEATS

ANSWERS . . . .

B) A Hammer

Believe it or not, hammer throwers regularly outdistance both shot putters and discuss throwers. Dwarf tossing has never been sanctioned as an Olympic event.

Source: *Encylcopaedia Britannica Almanac* (2003)

B) 19/1

Unless Page 3 girls are officially classified as sports stars, there seems little chance of the balance shifting – until WAGs form a competitive league.

Source: *Observer Sports Monthly* (May 2007)

C) 4/1

Fifty-one per cent of first goals are scored within 30 minutes of a game starting, while it is a 24/1 chance that the deadlock won't be broken until the last 10 minutes, and 11/1 that the match will end goalless.

Source: *Guardian* (17 March 2006)

ANSWERS ➤

Goalie Glory

IN WHAT percentage of football penalties will the taker's non-kicking foot point in the direction in which he is planning to hit the ball?

A) 85%   **B)** 60%   **C)** 40%

Nasser's Damned Unlucky

ENGLAND CRICKET captain Nasser Hussain skippered his country in 14 consecutive one-day internationals during 2000–01 and lost the toss in every one. What were the chances of that?

A) 179/1   **B)** 1,400/1   **C)** 16,383/1

Give Us a Break

WHAT PERCENTAGE of professional footballers are in favour of a two-week break during the season, provided it does not interfere with Christmas and New Year?

A) 0.3%   **B)** 27.2%   **C)** 72.5%

ANSWERS . . . .

A) 85%

In their book *How to Take a Penalty* Rob Eastaway and John Haigh reveal that 'one study discovered that 85% of the time the penalty taker's non-kicking foot points in the direction he is planning to kick the ball. If the goalkeeper can react quickly enough to this clue, his odds [of making a save] will improve.' Clearly the Germans have known this for some time.

Source: Rob Eastaway and John Haigh, *How to Take a Penalty* (Robson, 2005)

C) 16,383/1

Given that Hussain captained England 101 times throughout his career, there is a 179/1 chance that *at some stage* of those games he would endure a consecutive losing – or winning, for that matter – run of 14 tosses. However, to do so in that specific 14-match spell represented random odds of 16,383/1.

Source: Rob Eastaway and John Haigh, *How to Take a Penalty* (Robson, 2005)

C) 72.5%

In a survey of the Premiership, Championship, Leagues One and Two, 0.3% of the players polled said they didn't know! (It *is* a tough one: would you like a holiday?) Another 27.2% voted against such a break, but almost three-quarters were in favour. The highest vote in favour came from the Championship (81%), while the most anti were in League Two (38%).

Source: *Independent* (13 April 2006)

1 in 10? Not if Your Mate Kicks a Ball for a Living

WHAT PERCENTAGE of footballers from the top four English divisions say they have at least one gay friend?

A) 2%   **B)** 20%   **C)** 78%

Heaven Sent

BIRDIES ABOUND in pro golf tournaments the way bogeys do in the amateur ranks – almost routinely. For a pro, which of the following is most likely to be a 1 in 6,500 long shot?

A) Hole-in-One   **B)** Double Eagle   **C)** Lightning Strike

---

England Cap?

WHAT PERCENTAGE of footballers from the top four English divisions in 2006 were in favour of a salary cap that would prevent clubs from spending more than 75% of their income on their wage bills?

A) 3%   **B)** 39%   **C)** 58%

ANSWERS . . . .

B) 20%

Two per cent said they didn't know, while 20% said that they did have one or more. However, bucking every social survey of the last half-century or so, 78% claimed to have no gay friends whatsoever. As a follow-on question, they were asked, 'Is football a homophobic industry?' 3% didn't know; 40% said 'no'; and 57% said 'yes'. (But of the ones who said they had gay friends, 64.4% answered 'yes'.)

Source: *Independent* (13 April 2006)

A) Hole-in-One

The pros ace 1 in 6,500. By comparison, a double eagle is estimated at 1 in 6 million – the rarest in golf – in part, because most players can't reach a par five green in just two shots. A lightning strike, normally 1 in 550,000, could be almost a sure thing if you're one of those 'tough' guys who continue running around the course with metal sticks in their hands during a thunderstorm!

Source: PGW

C) 58%

Given that those quizzed were footballers earning an average £49,600 in League Two, £67,850 in One, £195,750 in the Championship and £676,000 in the Premiership, it may come as a surprise that so many were prepared to support the concept of a wage cap. Premiership footballers were the most in favour (with 64% of them supporting the idea), presumably because they've run out of space in their mansions to store their money.

Source: *Independent* (11 April 2006)

Losing Their Shirts . . . and Bras . . . and Pants

WHAT PERCENTAGE of online casino and poker players play in their underwear or completely naked?

A) 5%   **B)** 10%   **C)** 15%

Not So Golden Moments

WHAT WERE the odds that when Team GB won a medal at the 2004 Olympics in Athens, it would be bronze?

A) 6/4   **B)** 3/1   **C)** 6/1

What a Dope

WHAT ARE the odds of a UK athlete failing a test for a prohibited substance?

A) Almost 33/1   **B)** Almost 66/1   **C)** Almost 99/1

SPORTS: FEATS & DEFEATS

207

C) 15%

That means there might be as many as 225,000 gamblers playing their own, solitary version of strip poker. One on-line operator received such a positive response to its April Fool announcement that it planned to stage a naked tournament that it went ahead and did so for real. Over 150 turned up to play in the buff. For a change, they lost their shirts before even starting!

Source: *Online Gambler* magazine/InterCasino (February 2006)

A) 6/4

Of the 30 medals won by Britain in Athens, 9 were gold, 9 silver and 12 bronze. Kelly Holmes collected two of the Golds herself. It would be a bold tipster who predicted a higher tally for 2008 in Beijing.

C) Almost 99/1

Between 1999 and 2004, UK Sport carried out 29,114 tests for prohibited substances across 50 sports, which showed that 98.5% UK athletes are clean. Make up your own mind whether we should be proud of that, as it works out at over 400 athletes who failed the tests.

Source: *UK 2005*

WHAT ARE THE ODDS?

Life of Pie

ROTHERHAM Football Club was named the side where the greatest percentage of fans buy a pie when they go to matches. What percentage was that?

A) 20%   **B)** 40%   **C)** 60%

Pebble (Beach) Dash

AT THE inaugural London to Brighton car race in 1896, what were the odds of any one of the 39 competitors making it to the finish within the permitted time limit?

A) Zero   **B)** 2/1   **C)** 12/1

Gym'll Fix It?

IN AN international poll, what percentage of those questioned thought that gymnasts were the sexiest female sportspeople?

A) 23%   **B)** 31%   **C)** 58%

B) 40%

The average percentage of football fans treating themselves to a pie nationwide was 14–18%, but 40% of
fans visiting the Millmoor ground to watch Rotherham
play noshed down pies.

Source: 25th anniversary survey by Pukka Pies (2006)

B) 2/1

Given the fledgling nature of motor sport in those
days, for 13 to finish was no mean feat. But if they had
had speed cameras and traffic bumps to tackle, it may
have been substantially fewer.

C) 58%

Sprinters came in third, and tennis players were second, although it should be pointed out that the poll
was conducted in 1996, before the arrival of Anna
Kournikova or Maria Sharapova.

What's It All About, Alfie?

WHAT PERCENTAGE of internationals were won by the England football team when Alf Ramsey was in charge?

A) 33%   **B)** 50%   **C)** 60%

Twisted Minds

WHAT PERCENTAGE of people are supple enough to become professional contortionists?

A) 0.5%   **B)** 5%   **C)** 9.5%

Yeah, We Believe You

GOING INTO the 2006 World Cup, what were the odds that a Scotsman would be supporting England?

A) 4/1   **B)** Evens   **C)** 1/2

C) 60%

Sir Alf was the manager from 1963 to 1974 – this was in the days before you were called a turnip if you failed to win every game 3–0. But even if that had been the case, Alf might have lasted just as long. He sent out his side to play 113 matches, of which they lost just 17 and drew 27. That meant they had 69 victories (other sources suggested 68, with 28 draws) – a win percentage of just over 60% – one of which was achieved in extra time, against West Germany, in 1966. His teams scored 224 goals, conceding 99, making the average result a 2–1 victory.

Source: Niall Edworthy, *England: The Official FA History* (Virgin, 1997)

A) 0.5%

'I can do that – why do you think your Dad is still married to me?' said the mother of professional contortionist Amanda Grace when she, as a young girl, showed her Mum how flexible she was. Amanda now makes a living from her unusual ability, of which only 0.5% of the population shares.

Source: The Knowledge (17–23 June 2006)

C) 1/2

According to a survey conducted by the BBC, shortly before the World Cup in Germany got under way 25% of Scots were hoping that England would fail to win it, but 67% said they wanted the Auld Enemy to succeed. However, as just 5% of bets with British bookies for England to win were placed north of the border, one may suspect an element of political correctness.

Source: BBC TV (April 2006)

Sinical Tackle

WHAT PERCENTAGE of football fans support the introduction of the 'sin-bin' – a kind of midway point between yellow and red cards – into football?

A) 88%   **B)** 56%   **C)** 29%

Marathon Money

WHAT PERCENTAGE of the 34,500 runners in the 2006 London Marathon were fund-raising for charity?

A) 49%   **B)** 64%   **C)** 78%

Face Football Facts

WHICH FOOTBALLER topped a poll to find the ugliest player in the 2006 World Cup with 78% of the vote?

A) Frank Ribery   **B)** Cristiano Ronaldo
C) Wayne Rooney

213

B) 56%

When 43,000 suporters of Football League clubs were quizzed, 88% said they were in favour of the introduction of goal-line technology to check whether the ball had crossed the line. Presumably only 12% of those asked had memories stretching back to 1966, when England were helped out by a linesman standing 30 yards away but surely would have failed to score if the decision had been referred to a 'video referee'. Just over half favoured the introduction of a sin-bin punishment similar to the one already in use in rugby.

Source: British Football Week (25 April 2006)

C) 78%

From 10-foot giraffes to armour-clad St Georges, over three-quarters of the runners were raising cash for good causes. How come Paula Radcliffe never runs the race wearing, for example, a nurse's uniform? I, for one, would donate good money to see that.

Source: The Times (22 April 2006)

A) Frank Ribery

Rooney was the highest-placed Englishman in the vote, while Manchester United's Portuguese winger Ronaldo came in second, behind winner Ribery, the 27-year-old French winger.

Source: Daily Sport report on worldcup365.com poll (23 June , 2006)

WHAT ARE THE ODDS?

MIND ON
THE JOB

'All paid jobs absorb and degrade the mind.'
Aristotle (384–322 BC)

Mr Smith Will See You Now

WHEN YOU **arrive somewhere for an important meeting or appointment, what are the odds that the receptionist greeting you will be male?**

A) 13/1   **B)** 19/1   **C)** 33/1

You Learn Something Every Day

WHICH SUBJECT **attracted the biggest annual percentage increase in university applications in January 2006?**

A) Aerospace Engineering   **B)** Maths   **C)** Nursing

Nursed Out

WHAT ARE **the odds that a student nurse will quit before qualifying?**

A) 7/1   **B)** 5/1   **C)** 3/1

B) 19/1

Just 5% of receptionists in Britain's offices, dental surgeries and doctors' clinics are men, according to the Women's Equality Unit.

Source: *Guardian* (28 February 2006)

C) Nursing

Just 1.2% more applications were received for Aerospace Engineering while 11.5% more signed up for Maths. But Nursing showed a healthy rise of 15.4%. Let's hope there are enough hospitals open for them to work in.

Source: *Daily Mail* (16 February 2006)

C) 3/1

A study of 19,995 nursing students in 2004 revealed that 4,956, or 24.8%, dropped out before completing their course. The main reasons given were financial pressure, lack of childcare support and bad experiences on the ward.

Source: *Nursing Standard* magazine (2006)

WHAT ARE THE ODDS?

A Fair Cop?

WHAT ARE the odds that a police officer in
London will have a second job?

A) 1 in 15   **B)** 1 in 21   **C)** 1 in 29

_____

Brainbox

WHAT PERCENTAGE of Britons have an IQ of 148
or more?

A) 1%   **B)** 2%   **C)** 4%

_____

Wait a Minute!

WHAT PROPORTION of Eastern Europeans who
have arrived in Britain since 2004 are working
as waiters?

A) 20%   **B)** 12%   **C)** 7%

MIND ON THE JOB

219

ANSWERS . . . .

A) 1 in 15

You wouldn't think they had the time, would you?
However, 1,905 Met officers have business interests
outside their police work. In addition to keeping the
streets safe(ish), 4 serving officers were working as
models, 12 'provided massages', 4 hired out bouncy
castles, 17 dabbled in hypnotherapy and 2 were
florists!

Source: *Evening Standard* (31 December 2005)

B) 2%

According to Mensa – the organisation for super-brains
– the average IQ is 100, and only 1 in every 50 people
can boast an IQ of 148 or more. Madonna allegedly
comes in at a very respectable 140, while Carol
Vorderman is officially a genius with 157. Bill Clinton
reportedly claims a massive 182 – and he'd never lie,
would he?

Source: Mensa

C) 7%

It is estimated that more than 345,000 Eastern
Europeans have come to the UK seeking work since the
EU expanded to include former Soviet Bloc countries
on 1 May 2004. A huge 36% of them are currently
working in factories, 9% in warehouses and 9% as
packers. Just 7% are working as waiters, in spite of
what chef Antony Worrall Thompson, who was critical
of some of them in 2006, might think.

Source: Home Office (March 2006)

Missing You Already

WHAT PERCENTAGE of workers contact their
office whilst on holiday?

A) 38%   **B)** 40%   **C)** 56%

Self-Satisfaction

WHAT PROPORTION of UK workers are self-
employed?

A) 13%   **B)** 7%   **C)** 3%

Get Away From It All

WHAT PERCENTAGE of Britons would like to make
a fresh start by working abroad?

A) 12%   **B)** 16%   **C)** 45%

MIND ON THE JOB

221

C) 56%

Work obsessed, us? Some of this book was written around a pool, and researchers found that 38% of workers check office emails on their laptops whilst away, 40% read work reports, 56% can't resist checking up on what's happening back at work whilst sunning themselves on holiday.

Source: Survey by Virgin Holidays (2007)

A) 13%

That amounts to 3.6 million people, nearly three-quarters of them men, working for themselves in Britain. They are most likely to work in construction, banking, finance or insurance.

Source: *UK 2005*

A) 12%

45% of those surveyed wanted a career break so that they could travel, but intended to come back once they had got it out of their system; 12% wanted to work abroad; and 16% wanted to retrain.

Source: *Evening Standard* (20 March 2006)

Working Mums

WHAT ARE the odds that a mother of children under five will also have a full- or part-time job?

A) 5/6   **B)** 2/1   **C)** 3/1

Writing on the Wall?

WHAT PERCENTAGE of the population regularly write letters or notes?

A) 13%   **B)** 26%   **C)** 39%

Wots the Nswr?

WHAT ARE the odds that a child caught cheating in a GCSE or A level exam was using a mobile phone to do so?

A) Evens   **B)** 3/1   **C)** 9/1

MIND ON THE JOB

ANSWERS . . . .

A) 5/6

Eleven per cent of women aged between 16 and 64 are
without work because they are looking after their families or their home, while 55% of mothers with children
under five now hold down a full- or part-time job. In
total 70% of women are in work.

Source: Office for National Statistics (March 2006)

A) 13%

With everyone texting or emailing, cheques disappearing, and credit cards not even requiring a signature
since the advent of 'chip-and-pin', 87% of the population are probably losing the ability to write their
names, let alone anything else. However, 40% of pensioners still scribble letters and notes regularly.

Source: Institute of Practitioners in Advertising (March 2006)

B) 3/1

Of the 4,547 youngsters discovered cheating in the
summer of 2005 (up from 3,573 the previous year), 1
in 4 was disqualified for using a mobile phone in the
exam hall. There was a 450/1 chance (nine people were
caught doing it) that the disqualification was for
impersonating the person who should have been sitting the exam.

Source: Qualifications and Curriculum Authority (March 2006)

Fat's Just Not Fair

WHAT ARE the odds that a recruitment professional will not employ an obese worker for fear
that he or she will take too much time off sick?

A) 2/1 **B)** 3/1 **C)** 4/1

Clean Baffled

WHAT PROPORTION of British men cannot work
out how to use a washing machine?

A) 1 in 10 **B)** 1 in 15 **C)** 1 in 20

Spam, Spam, Spam, Spam . . .

WHAT PERCENTAGE of all emails are spam?

A) 3.8% **B)** 13.3% **C)** 60%

MIND ON THE JOB

225

B) 3/1

A survey of 500 recruitment professionals found that 11% of them believed it was reasonable to sack a worker for being obese. And even though employers could be breaking the law by refusing a job to someone merely because of the fear of future health problems, about 1 in 4 managers said that they try to avoid taking on obese employees. My philosophy is that I'll hire anyone who knows what obese means and can spell it.

Source: John Hardman & Co. (March 2006)

A) 1 in 10

And it gets worse, because while most men claimed that they could work the things, 55% of them admitted that they had ruined clothes at one time or another, which we reckon means they don't really know how to use them at all. As someone who once set a tumble dryer ablaze when trying to dry a football kit, I have no intention of endeavouring to master the mysteries of washing machines.

Source: Comet (April 2006)

C) 60%

Every second, 3.8 cans of Spam are consumed in the USA, but that has nothing to do with the fact that the average employee receives 13.3 items of electronic irritation every day, comprising three out of every five emails that are delivered.

Source: *The Indypedia* (2006)

WHAT ARE THE ODDS?

Reflecting on Ladder-related Catastrophes

WHICH OF these is the most widely accepted superstition in Britain?

A) Seeing a Black Cat   **B)** Breaking a Mirror
C) Walking Under a Ladder

_____

Bleeding Hell!

WHAT ARE the odds that someone aged under 30 will know how to bleed a radiator?

A) 4/5   **B)** 2/1   **C)** 10/1

_____

Sky Low

WHAT PERCENTAGE of over-50s cannot set up a VCR, DVD or Sky+ box?

A) 18%   **B)** 36%   **C)** 54%

MIND ON THE JOB

227

C) **Walking Under a Ladder**

Sixty-seven per cent were convinced that *something* happened when they saw a black cat, but they were far from sure of what exactly, with some thinking it was good luck while others believed it was bad. Just 54% thought it was unlucky to break a mirror, but 83% skirted around ladders to avoid misfortune. Superstition is all nonsense, say I, touch wood.

Source: Folklore Society (1998)

A) **4/5**

That translates to 56% of them claiming to know how to do it. Do we believe them? Here's some more information that might help you decide. Only 51% of under-30s can hang wallpaper, 27% of them cannot sew a hem and 26% of them are unable to wire a plug. In contrast, 74% of over-50s can hang wallpaper, just 14% of them have trouble with hems and only 6% of them are bewildered by plugs. What's a plug?

Source: Direct Line Home Response 24 (April 2006)

A) **18%**

In contrast, only 4% of the under-30s have similar problems. Clearly this is why so many of them have trouble with bleeding radiators – they're too busy reading bleeding instruction manuals. The over-50s are similarly befuddled by flatpack furniture, with 16% of them unable to assemble it, against only 7% of the under-30s.

Source: Direct Line Home Response 24 (April 2006)

Fair Cop?

WHAT PROPORTION of policemen cleared to carry on working within the force will have been convicted or cautioned for minor assault or minor damage?

A) 17%   **B)** 30%   **C)** 50%

Cyber-Socialising

WHAT PERCENTAGE of workers admitted to spending more time emailing socially than working whilst at the office?

A) 83%   **B)** 43%   **C)** 19%

Dream Nightmare

WHAT PERCENTAGE of Britons have been upset with someone they know because of abuse they have received from them ... in a dream?

A) 4.5%   **B)** 18.8%   **C)** 21.5%

MIND ON THE JOB

A) 17%

Apparently 'dozens' of police officers with criminal convictions are employed by Scotland Yard, according to Met Police Commissioner Ian Blair. In total, 74 officers who had broken the law between 2000 and 2005 had been cleared by the Metropolitan Police to carry on working. Of those, 61 had been convicted of drink-driving, while all the rest had been convicted or cautioned for 'minor' assault or criminal damage.

Source: *Daily Mail* (11 April 2006)

B) 43%

83% admitted that they lost vital work data from their computers because they were cyber-socialising, while 43% owned up to spending more time socialising online than working.

Source: Survey of 1,000 workers by computer company Hewlett Packard (2006)

B) 18.8%

A survey of 3,000 people revealed that over a third of Britons 'have made a dramatic life-changing decision after interpreting or acting out a dream'. An astonishing 4.5% of people have discovered that they have had the same dream on the same night as someone they know; 21.5% dream of imaginary characters; while nearly 20% get the hump when someone they know has been nasty to them in their dream.

Source: *Daily Express* (15 April 2006)

Cheering News

HOW MUCH **more or less intelligent are women who drink up to two glasses of wine a day compared with those who drink none at all or very little?**

A) 20% Less   **B)** Identical   **C)** 20% More

No Time for Tea

WHAT PERCENTAGE **of office workers no longer take the traditional 'tea-break'?**

A) 10%   **B)** 56%   **C)** 63%

Stressed Out

DESPITE THEIR **apparently comfortable salary, what percentage of men earning over £50,000 per annum suffer from 'moderate to extreme' stress on a weekly basis?**

A) 31%   **B)** 59%   **C)** 93%

MIND ON THE JOB

ANSWERS . . . .

C) 20% More

According to a study of 2,215 people, women who had a couple of glasses of wine each day (which is considerably more than the recommended daily amount in guidelines issued by the government) scored about 20% higher in intelligence tests than those who were teetotal or drank very little. Unfortunately, the researchers said that they could not carry out a similar test of men, because they had 'great trouble finding male teetotallers who could provide a sober benchmark'!

Source: *Stroke: Journal of the American Heart Association* (April 2006)

B) 56%

Ten per cent of office workers say that they don't take tea- or coffee-breaks any more because their boss or colleagues disapprove, while 46% no longer do so because 'they think it will look bad or feel they will let others down'. In contrast, prior to the 1 July 2007 smoking ban, 63% of office workers who were smokers were quite happy to stop at regular intervals throughout the day for a puff, apparently unable to care less what their colleagues or bosses thought.

Source: Fabulous Bakin' Boys (April 2006)

B) 59%

Given that one might reasonably believe that enviable financial reward will probably involve an element of stress as par for the course, that figure is perhaps lower than one might expect. Perhaps the other 41% just don't know they are stressed – or aren't good enough to ever induce stress. 31% said they coped with stress by going to bed early.

Source: Study by You Gov for Men's Health Forum (June 2006)

IT'S
SHOWBIZ
TIME

'Sometimes you have to let people down to get on, particularly in showbusiness.'

Dusty Springfield

Keeping Up With the Jones

WHAT PERCENTAGE of women said that the woman whose body they most admired was that of Catherine Zeta-Jones?

A) 5.6% **B)** 18.2% **C)** 37.4%

Not So Merry Christmas

WHAT PERCENTAGE of festive shoppers voted 'I Wish It Could Be Christmas Every Day' as the most irritating Christmas song?

A) 15.38% **B)** 21.05% **C)** 33.33%

Rise and Shine

JUST WHAT percentage of the vote did Eamonn Holmes and Fiona Phillips garner in a poll to find British viewers' favourite ever breakfast TV presenters?

A) 24% **B)** 48% **C)** 72%

IT'S SHOWBIZ TIME

C) 37.4%

Victoria Beckham's body won the approval of 5.6% of those women polled, with Kate Moss stacking up 18.2%, but Catherine Zeta-Jones was the runaway winner.

Source: Survey of 2,055 female readers of *You* magazine (December 2006)

C) 33.33%

The poll by eBuyer in 2005 saw Paul McCartney take 3rd place with 'Wonderful Christmas Time', nominated by 15% of those surveyed. Shakin' Stevens came 2nd, with 21%, for 'Merry Christmas Everyone'. But Wizzard cantered home with 1 out of every 3 votes cast. Astonishingly, Cliff Richard's 'Mistletoe and Wine' was only 4th. Bah, humbug!

Source: *Daily Star* (16 February 2005)

A) 24%

Eamonn and Fiona topped the list. In 2nd place were Johnny Vaughan and Denise Van Outen, who scored 11% in spite of their later efforts to 'entertain' us on a Saturday evening. Selina Scott and Frank Bough came in 3rd, with 8%. Chris Evans and Gaby Roslin received just 7%, while Nick Owen and Anne Diamond got only 6%.

Source: *Daily Mirror* (20 February 2006)

Trust Me

WHO CAME **top in a national survey to find out
which public figure was most trusted by
Britons?**

A) Rolf Harris   **B)** Sir Trevor McDonald
C) Sir David Attenborough

Role Over

IN **2006, 777 'young people' (aged between 16
and 19) were asked for their role models. Who
came top?**

A) J. K. Rowling   **B)** Richard Branson
C) David Beckham

Ninny Versus Winnie

IN A **2006 poll to name their 'all-time inspira-
tional hero', what were the odds that any of the
18,862 people who took part nominated
Celebrity *Big Brother*'s Chantelle?**

A) 33/1   **B)** 678/1   **C)** 2,357/1

IT'S SHOWBIZ TIME

237

C) **Sir David Attenborough**

Rolf, bless him and his didgeridoo, was 3rd; while Sir Trev came in 2nd. Notable others in the list were Tony Blair, who was 79th (why so high?), and the Queen, who finished 13th. Given Sir Dave's domination, one wonders whether animals were permitted to vote.

Source: *Daily Mirror* (26 January 2006)

B) **Richard Branson**

Hmm, you have to wonder where those 777 were questioned. On a flight to New York, perhaps? Maybe in Virgin as they were buying the new Robbie Williams CD? Anyway, Becks came 3rd and J. K. was runner-up.

Source: YouGov

C) **2,357/1**

Winston Churchill romped to victory in the poll, with 10% of the vote, finishing ahead of runner-up Nelson Mandela and 3rd-placed Martin Luther King. Chantelle inspired eight people to vote for her, although it is unclear whether they had to get someone else to fill out the form for them. 'It must be distressing to us all that eight Britons were inspired by her above Winston and Nelson,' reflected *The Times*. Ah, yes, but at least Chantelle never ordered the bombing of Dresden, did she?

Source: AOL (March 2006)

WHAT ARE THE ODDS?

Would You Beeblieve It?

WHICH BBC station has the biggest share of the radio audience?

A) Radio 1   **B)** Radio 2   **C)** Radio 4

Girl Power

WHAT PERCENTAGE of Britons chose the Spice Girls as the biggest cultural icons of the 1990s?

A) 80%   **B)** 50%   **C)** 20%

I Do!

WHAT WERE the odds of a contestant on *Who Wants to Be a Millionaire?* winning the jackpot, as of March 2006?

A) 282/1   **B)** 11,132/1   **C)** 1,000,000/1

IT'S SHOWBIZ TIME

239

B) Radio 2

With 53.1% of the UK radio audience choosing a BBC station, 8.3% opted for 1; 16.2% for 2; 1.1% for 3; 11% for 4; and 4.5% for 5. Of the rest, 10% went for regional stations and just 0.6% for arguably the best of the lot, the BBC's World Service.

Source: Radio Authority Joint Audience Research (2006)

A) 80%

In a poll of 1,000 people for Trivial Pursuit, carried out in March 2006, 8 out of 10 voted for Posh, Ginger and, er, the other three; 46% chose Quentin Tarantino's *Pulp Fiction* as the most memorable film, while the Millennium Dome was labelled the most memorable mistake of the decade.

Source: Trivial Pursuit Poll

A) 282/1

In total, 1,132 people had been in the hot seat on the 412 shows up to the end of March 2006. Garden designer Judith Keppel, teacher David Edwards, banker Robert Brydges and computer software designer Pat Gibson made off with the million. We have not included Major Charles Ingram in our list of winners because, while he managed to give the correct answer to the big question, the programme never coughed up the cash.

Source: *Daily Express* (31 March 2006)

Lookalikeabecks

WHAT ARE the odds that a Briton will try to look like his or her celebrity hero or heroine?

A) 2/1   **B)** 4/1   **C)** 8/1

Can I Have More Jamie, Please?

WHAT PERCENTAGE of Britons said the celebrity they most envied was Jamie Oliver?

A) 7%   **B)** 9%   **C)** 12%

Who's the Daddy?

WHO TOPPED a poll to discover the 'Best Celebrity Dad'?

A) David Beckham   **B)** Bob Geldof   **C)** Jamie Oliver

IT'S SHOWBIZ TIME

241

B) 4/1

In a poll of 4,000 people a startling 1 in 5 admitted to trying to copy the wardrobes and lifestyles of their role models. Top for men, predictably, was David Beckham, which explains the great sarong shortage of 1999. Perhaps a tad more surprising is that Dawn French is the most imitated female role model, which might explain the great Terry's Chocolate Orange shortage of 2004.

Source: *People* (2 April 2006)

C) 12%

Among 1,000 people polled in a survey to mark National Identity Fraud Prevention Week (is it just me, or is there now a week for absolutely everything?), Bob Geldof attracted 7% of the vote; 9% opted for David Beckham and Robbie Williams each; but the cheeky chirpy chappie chef came top of the list. Highest-ranked female celeb was Angelina Jolie, with 8%, almost entirely because of who she gets to go to bed with every night, we imagine.

Source: Yahoo Entertainment News (18 October 2005)

B) Bob Geldof

Presumably you have to give your child a ridiculous name before you can even be considered a 'celebrity dad'. Anyway, Jamie came 3rd, with 15% of the vote for the way he is bringing up Daisy Boo and Poppy Honey. Becks got 20% for being so kind to Brooklyn, Romeo and Cruz. But Bob Geldof ran off with the laurels, polling 23%, for the great job he's done with Pixie and Peaches. We're guessing Chris Martin was deemed ineligible because Apple just isn't ludicrous enough.

Source: *Sun* (11 April 2006)

The Sex Factor

WHO TOPPED a 2006 poll to find the man British women would most like to find under the duvet?

A) Simon Cowell   **B)** Robbie Williams
C) David Beckham

Hoff We Go

WHAT ARE the odds of former Baywatch star David Hasselhoff being the male celebrity most gossiped about via email?

A) 9.6%   **B)** 23.1%   **C)** 30%

Sharp Rebuke

IN A SURVEY of the 100 most annoying things, what are the odds of a celebrity having being chosen?

A) 6/1   **B)** 12/1   **C)** 16/1

IT'S SHOWBIZ TIME

243

ANSWERS ·

A) Simon Cowell

Yes, that really does say 'Simon Cowell'. Becks came in only 4th, with 12% of the vote. Ahead of him, with 18.9%, was the new James Bond, Daniel Craig. Robbie was runner-up, with 20%, but the prince of the high-waisted trousers topped the list, with 21%.

Source: Silentnight (May 2006)

C) 30%

It transpires that Hasselhoff has won an award for being the most watched TV star in the world, so topping the list of gossiped-about celebs in emails is no great surprise. Modestly, 'The Hoff' commented: 'I'm delighted to be such a hit on the web and to be crowned king of the Internet.'

Source: *Sun* (26 June, 2006)

B) 12/1

While Craig David came in at number 93, Natasha Kaplinsky at 77, Russell Brand at 69 and David Blaine at 47, the rest of the celebs featured made it into the Top 20. With Abi Titmuss nestling at 18 and Carol Vorderman at a lofty 12, Chantelle and Preston were together voted in at number 8, while James Blunt was the most annoying of the lot in the poll topped by cold callers, caravans and queue jumpers.

Source: Survey of 2050 adults for Lactofree (July 2006)